So Worth More

Jax Stuart

Copyright

Dedication

For my first year English teacher, Mr Glass, who gave me encouragement at such an important time in my life. I never forgot his enthusiasm for my scribbled words.

Be what you wish

Sarah J Maas

Many Thanks

To my kids and husband, thank you for letting me actually write and being interested in the whole process.

Thank you to Kelly for the names and encouragement over the months. I could do without all the plot bunnies - kidding! Danielle for always wanting to read it. Kristen, my proof reader and dear friend for all the work. Rachele being willing to read it even though it's a romance!

My Alphas, Rye, Liz, Janet and Annie for all the suggestions. Apologies again for how rough it was! It got there eventually. You were all so helpful.

My fantastic betas, Sarah, Haylee and Carolina for that last push to make it as good as I could and for sorting name mix ups!

A shout out to Cameron Craig for the advice. Us baby authors have to stick together and it's great to have the support.

Thanks also to Amanda Cashure,Sterling Thomas and Stella Rainbow for the advice.

Many thanks to the MM romance community who have been so welcoming, the authors on Discord that ran sprints with me and everyone that gave a kind word when self doubt got in the way.

A thanks to Covers by Jo for my fantastic cover!

A final thank you to the readers. I really appreciate you taking a chance on me.

One - Andy

Water streamed down my body, rinsing away sweat from an intense workout. Feeling a draft, I paused washing, turned my head and caught the sound of the shower curtain being pulled aside. I heard the rustle of clothing before I was roughly turned around and pushed against the tiled wall. A familiar mouth firmly covered mine. Half-heartedly, I tried to pull away, to push Will back, but the heavier man didn't budge.

"Not here," I panted against Will's neck even as I pushed my lower body against his, desperate for the feel of him, noticing how hard he was. "We almost got banned last time," I whispered. Outside of the stall, I could hear the sounds of other people showering off their own workouts on both sides of us. Will pulled back a couple of inches and smirked, his brown eyes alight with mischief while he ran his hands down my back and roughly grabbed at my ass.

"Worth it, though. How about we skip drinks with the guys and head back to yours?" he growled out, his voice doing nothing for my paper-thin control. Will crowded in close again. He dipped his head, water running over his dark hair, and started tracing kisses along my collarbone in the way that he knew drove me crazy. Drawing them up over my neck, all the while thrusting his cock against mine. Despite knowing we could get caught, and that this was a terrible idea, I could feel my orgasm approaching. His kisses paused as he said against my jaw, voice tight with desire, "I need you in a bed. Now."

The alarm blaring from my phone was never welcome, but even less so this morning after that dream. Although it wasn't really a dream but more of an amalgamation of every time I'd been with Will over the last four months. The temptation to just pull the covers over my head and take a sick day was so strong.

Friday had really done a number on me, it seemed. After each encounter I swore it would be the last. That I deserved better than being Will's fuck-toy. Realistically, I knew that I didn't mean anything more to Will than a convenient form of stress relief. This was par for the course for me. We weren't friends. We didn't communicate outside of work and the gym, and it was really starting to get to me. I felt cheap, especially after the way I'd been treated over the weekend. You'd think I'd be used to the way guys treated me by now. Like I was either disposable or they owned me. There was no in between.

I'd thought Will might be different, but no. Sure, he'd been clear about what we were, but there were so many blurred lines and unspoken rules to what we were doing. Breaking one had serious consequences, mainly for me, since they were Will's rules, not mine. Except each time he hurt me I knew it was my fault because I was letting him and somehow I always forgave him and got sucked back in. It was emotionally exhausting, and I needed to stop the cycle before I really got hurt. Again.

The erection I'd woken with had softened when I recalled the look in Will's eyes the last time I'd caught him looking at me before he fled from my apartment. He'd actually knocked into the furniture in a rare show of clumsiness in his haste to leave.

Letting out a sigh, resigned to actually getting out of bed and facing the music, I rolled out of my rumpled bed and headed across the studio apartment to the tiny bathroom to shower. The water pressure sucked compared to that of the gym and Will's apartment, not that I should be having showers at a hookup's place, I reminded myself with an eye roll. A message that I'd gotten clearly the one and only time I'd accidentally fallen asleep at Will's and had to deal with the fallout. Groaning, frustrated that my thoughts were still stuck on him, I rested my head against the damp off-white tiles and gave myself a talking to. Will was a bad habit, an addiction, and one I needed to give up for my sanity.

While I got ready for work, I continued to brace myself for the day. Mondays were the worst with Will. He was always colder than usual after a weekend's closeness, and Friday's fuck-up pretty much ensured that this week was going to be extra weird. Touching Will in front of the other guys at the bar we frequented after our workouts shouldn't have meant anything in normal circles, but I'd seen the knowing glances that Pete, Henry, and Brad had shared. I could still feel Will tense up under my hand when he'd noticed them and remembered my feeling of apprehension. Not that I was scared of Will. Yes, he was a few inches bigger than my five nine, and quite a bit broader in the shoulders and chest, but I didn't think that he would physically hurt me. Except that night Will had been rougher than normal, though I didn't mind a little rough handling. He'd been less playful and more about his own pleasure, escaping out the door before the cum had cooled on the sheets. Not that he usually lingered long after, *and he certainly didn't cuddle,* I thought with a frown. Why did I let him treat me like dirt? Was great sex worth feeling like shit after? Was my self-worth really so low?

I scoffed at my thoughts as I grabbed a clean, pale blue shirt from my closet and started to dress for work, grabbing a pair of navy pants and matching tie as well. While this place was small and outdated, it was cheap and a convenient distance from the office so I could walk when the weather was good. It also benefited from decent storage space and had everything I really needed. It was probably the place I'd lived at the longest since my mom's house. The apartment had become my safe haven and it had to have been kismet that I'd found it. There weren't so many places that were close to work and within my limited budget before my promotion. I'd been gutted when there was a time when I thought I might have to move. Especially after working so hard to make it a home.

My king-sized bed was against one wall in the corner of the apartment. My flat screen TV, a promotion splurge, was on the opposite wall with a cheap worn coffee table and blue couch in front of it. Abigail, my twin, had seen the state of the couch I'd found at a Goodwill one time she had visited and freaked out, refusing to sit on it. Days later she had reappeared with a stack of fabric and her beloved sewing machine, and covered it with a cheery handmade blue throw that managed to compliment the original blue fabric of the couch, and then had made some silver cushions. This was after she had made me steam clean the thing. My lips lifted in a smile at the thought of my sister and her bossy ways.

After negotiating a reduction in my monthly rent in exchange for us improving the place, Abby had made it her mission to make it less of a "hovel", as she called it. The small kitchen had been given a face-lift when she'd found these stickers that looked like wood to cover the cabinets and then installed new handles, somehow making the cabinets look new. Together, we had refinished the counter-top, which had been a production and a half that involved us falling out briefly, and me storming out of my own apartment to go to a bar to have a few shots before coming home to apologize with a bottle of wine for my put-upon twin.

On a vacation from work, being unable to afford to go anywhere, I'd hired a carpet cleaner from the local grocery store and washed the faded brown carpet three times before admitting defeat on some of the stains. The landlord wouldn't replace the carpet, much to Abby's disdain, so she had found me a silver and blue rug that hid the worst of the marks. Then she'd given up her time to help me repaint the place a light gray. She'd said, "Andy, you may live in a dump, but it just needs some work and some love." I'd never admit that she was right. I loved the place it had become. It wasn't much, but it was home.

Finishing dressing, I crossed to the tiny kitchen and pushed the button on my baby. The coffee machine had been a real splurge, but I had just finished a huge project in the months before Will's arrival in the office, and the bonus had covered it. It was a real treat, since my budget could be a little tight. A Black Friday deal helped with the eye-watering cost, and the rest of that much deserved check had gone into my savings. Mom had always taught us to have a back-up plan.

Pouring a large mug and doctoring it to my taste with vanilla flavored creamer, I pondered breakfast choices instead of the day ahead. Too much focus on that and I'd lose my appetite, and a busy Monday on an empty stomach was a bad idea. As I drank my coffee and made some toast, I checked the weather report on my phone; the chance of rain was too high, so I decided to take the car.

Finishing up with plenty of time before I actually had to be at work left too much time to think and had my anxiety building. *Fuck it, just go in early and get started on something,* I thought to myself. Snatching up my faux leather messenger bag (a gift from a previous client) from the floor next to the couch and my keys from the blue glass bowl on the console table next to the door (thank you Abs), I headed out to the parking garage. Getting into my boring older model silver sedan (hello cheap and cheerful!), I took a couple of seconds to hook my phone up to the stereo and found my power play list full of, frankly, some cheesy pop, and attempted to get with the program.

Will - bad, distance - good. No more hooking up. No more games. *Yeah right!* the voice in the back of my head scoffed. Sometimes that voice sounded suspiciously like Will.

***

Determined that this Monday would not be full of hollow promises like the Mondays that preceded it since Will had joined the company, I vowed to stay firm and not give into our messed up dynamic. Usually I'd be firm with myself all weekend, the same as all the weekends before it. Normally I would get ready to go into the office, and I'd attempt to put whatever plan I'd hastily drawn up that particular weekend into action. I would be determined. Except I was hurt this week; Will had acted like a dick. Admittedly the dream had thrown me a little with a reminder of our explosive chemistry, a glimpse of how good it was with Will, but that blip was over, I attempted to assure myself.

Yet I wasn't sure I could hold myself to all those promises I'd made.

Even as I parked, I was already giving into the temptation to play the same silly games with Will. Unable to resist poking the bear. I found myself smiling as I snagged the space assigned for the project manager that'd been allotted before there was a need for two teams and two managers. The idea was to take turns using the space, but every day was a fight over it. My seniority from being with the company for the last seven years apparently meant nothing to Will, who deemed himself more important than me somehow, as he'd brought some big name clients to Parker's Advertising and PR with him.

Usually there was also the mad dash to the elevator if we arrived at the same time, neither of us undignified enough to make a run for it, but moving quickly across the garage, making sure the elevator doors closed on a furious face because of course we couldn't share the elevator! *What would people think?* I thought, rolling my eyes. There was no need this morning for my signature smirk when the doors invariably closed on Will. Being that bit smaller had its perks for sure - I was fast.

The rest of the usual routine was taking the last of the coffee in the pot and reorganizing the perfectly configured (to Will's preference, of course) shared desk. Not today though, I wasn't falling into bad habits. Generally, it was a case of doing anything to get a rise out of my desk mate. Childish, I know, but it was my way of leveling the playing field. It annoyed me that I was already failing just by picking the parking space instead of parking literally anywhere else. So after pouring my cup, I set up a new pot so there'd be fresh coffee for Will. I let out a small sigh.

Often I found myself wondering what would happen if one of us didn't play the game. Would that be enough to change things up? Could we build an actual friendship? We had plenty in common on the surface. We just liked to piss each other off. It was like foreplay drawn out over the week, seeing who would slip first.

For someone who had their life together as much as I seemed to on the outside, inside sure felt like a mess. I honestly hated playing these games, but Will couldn't give me anything real even if that was what I truly wanted from him. We appeared to be stuck in this cycle.

Sitting back in my chair sipping coffee, I noticed Will approach, face like a thundercloud as he took a seat at our shared desk with a bitter sigh even though he held a fresh coffee from the pot I'd made.

Looking away, I felt a prickle of guilt flow through me, which also kinda pissed me off. But I'd vowed to stop trying to wind Will up. So what if I'd gotten the parking space today? He could have it tomorrow. I hadn't done anything else, having realized that it wasn't too late to change things up since Will had been later getting in than me. *So far so good*, I thought, aside from the wave of tension from Will. I went to speak to him but noticing his glower, I decided against it. I'd let him stew a bit; maybe he'd notice I wasn't bringing anything up and things would be okay. *As if,* my inner voice mocked.

As project managers, we may have shared desk space to "collaborate" but we each ran our own team of preferred artists and copy editors, only pulling together on rare projects that required it. This meant for large parts of the day we could be away from the desk overseeing projects. Much easier for avoiding the usual arguments or baiting.

Ignoring Will, I got up to put my empty mug in the break room and check on Jenny, Clara, and her wife, Suneya in the art circle. Largely, Will's team ran different hours to mine, with my own team preferring to start their day earlier so they could work in the quiet of the office at any of the projects they were working on and have an early finish. Will's team usually started at least an hour after mine with Will only starting that bit earlier to do admin, the same things that I often found myself doing at home. Normally this was great and meant the office was quiet. Today though, it made it uncomfortable.

The air was filled with tension and I could see that Clara, the de facto leader of the group, wanted to ask what was going on. Looking at her with a serious expression, I gave her a subtle shake of my head and quickly glanced at Will, who had turned his back on them.

Aside from our games, Will and I usually managed to be civil and professional while working, after the initial bumps, that is. We didn't have to like each other to work well together. We at least had respect for each other's abilities. Or at least I know I did. Will was talented, no doubt, and while we had issues outside of work, I admired how Will ran his projects. Today though, that professional veneer was slipping.

The day progressed almost like a normal Monday, except that I used every opportunity to avoid the shared desk like the thing was going to bite me. I chose to work in the art circle, picking up an art tablet or sitting down with the copy editors and drawing up slogans instead. At one point, I even went up to the PR floor rather than sending an email and had a chat with Jeremy about where they wanted an ongoing campaign to go.

Lunch was spent out at a cafe with my tablet instead of ordering in and eating at our desk. There was no chance of me using the men's room at the end of the hall and risking getting cornered. I'd learned that lesson... eventually, anyway. Will seemed to thaw over the day as I gave him space. We'd had arguments before during our "thing" or whatever it was, but this time I was done and until I worked up the courage to tell him, it was best to avoid any situations where we could be alone.

Picking up my phone at the end of the day, having avoided the thing as much as the desk, I saw a message from Will that I promptly ignored, not ready to deal with it. Instead, I flicked the notifications away and opened up the gym's app. In order to successfully dodge Will, I'd need to change up my gym routine, and the yoga class that started in forty-five minutes would be a perfect escape.

Thank god there was no chance of Will attending it, because I needed a good stretch and workout. Anxiety over the weekend had my muscles feeling tight and prickly.

My phone buzzed in my hand with another message from Will. I hovered over the reply button for a minute before going into the chat and muting it for a day. Maybe then Will would get the hint, or maybe I'd finally feel brave enough to say something to him. I wanted to believe that my resolve would hold, but I'd been close to pulling the plug before and folded.

For a second I thought about blocking him, but occasionally there was work stuff that came up that we had to talk about, and in all honesty, I knew that I really should say something to Will, redefine this thing, but it was just a bit raw for me today. Maybe tomorrow.

***

Tuesday was much the same as Monday and Clara had gotten me alone to ask what was going on as the atmosphere had gotten worse in the office. Will's face was stuck in what appeared to be a permanent glare. Somehow the unapproachable air and bad attitude made him hotter. He growled at the Tuesday check in meeting instead of speaking, which had me half hard for most of the morning when I thought about it. Will's team was even looking to me for answers. I had managed to fob Clara off with "nothing much, just a difference of opinion," which she only frowned at. My weak attempt at keeping it vague seemed to leave Clara with more questions.

No one at work knew about us hooking up. It was one of Will's rules, which I had actually agreed with since it wasn't anyone's business but ours. We'd worried that we would lose the respect of the staff. Our rivalry was often the target of many jokes, my colleagues joking about our apparent love/hate relationship and often we took part, making probably horribly inappropriate murder jokes. At least we did when Will wasn't freaking out over an innocent shoulder touch and some pretty on the nose assumptions from our shared friends.

Taking a minute to get myself together, I decided to grab another coffee in the break room and message Will back. I hadn't read any of the messages that Will had sent, knowing that it was likely to be baseless accusations and then some cajoling. Apologies for overreacting were unlikely so I continued to ignore them and quickly drafted a message.

Andy: I think that what we've been doing is a mistake and we should stop. Don't contact me unless it's about work, okay? I think some space is a good idea.

My gut clenched with anxiety as I waited for a response. I didn't have to wait long, as around half a minute later came the reply.

Will: Fine.

Fine? He thought it was fine? After months of this, *that* was his response? I let out a huff of annoyance while running a hand through my dark blond hair, tugging at the slightly over-long strands in frustration. My eyes narrowed, I watched Will from the doorway of the break room as he got up from his side of the desk, grabbed his things and stormed out of the office without a backwards glance. Sure he was fine, alright.

Two - Will

The office bustled around me while frustration boiled inside; granted there was also a sliver of guilt prickling at me, but mostly it was anger. Yesterday in the office was so uncomfortable. Rationally, I knew that I'd overreacted with Andy on Friday. Why I had gone home with him that night when internally I'd been freaking out, half of me just wanting to flee, I didn't know.

Having spent all weekend and yesterday thinking about things, I knew that I'd been rougher than I'd intended, not that Andy didn't like it a little rougher on occasion, but this was beyond that. I'd been selfish, taking what I wanted and that sense of shame that made me flee still came to the forefront of my brain when I thought of it. I'd treated Andy like a hump and dump, which he didn't deserve. That I knew for sure. Unfortunately I didn't seem to know how to apologize and redraw boundaries because it sure looked like Andy needed a reminder. We might both hang out with the guys, but we weren't friends, we couldn't be. Andy didn't fit in my world, in my life. He'd be chewed up and spat out. He was too nice. Too normal. So, co-workers and gym buddies only, a hook up, and absolutely not a boyfriend.

Just thinking of the way the guys had looked at us with knowing glances got me riled up again and I clenched my fists under the desk, taking a couple of deep breaths to calm me down. Andy was great in bed, and out of it. *If those shower stalls at the gym could talk,* I thought to myself with a quick grin. Possibly the best sex I'd ever had. We were compatible in the bedroom at least, and had great chemistry, but that's all there was to us, it was superficial. There wasn't anything extra I could give him. More to the point, as cold as it might sound, I didn't want to. I preferred having something quick and easy, no strings, no commitments, just decent sex when I wanted it and I didn't see that changing. It wasn't hurting anyone. I thought the whole point of having rules was to keep us on the same page, that way there weren't any expectations of anything I couldn't give. I didn't want to hurt Andy. As much as the guy bugged me at times, I knew he was a decent person. *Far too good for the likes of you really,* my inner voice snarked at me.

Andy wouldn't even look at me though, and resisted any attempts at conversation. He wouldn't answer any of my messages. I'd tried not to hound him, not wanting to look desperate, but I knew that we had to clear the air. I didn't think I'd be able to relax properly, take that weight off, until I knew we were okay.

There was a buzzing sound from my pocket and I grabbed out my phone to see a text from Andy. *Finally*! Except, instead of relief, I felt anger boil over inside of me as I read the text. *A mistake?* My thoughts kept tripping on those words even as I typed my reply. It was time to go before I said something, did something, that I would regret. Normally I was far more even tempered, but this whole situation had me on a knife edge and I really didn't want to lose this job. Gathering up my stuff, I stalked out of the office, forcing myself not to look for Andy before I left.

Rounding the corner quickly, I slammed into someone. "Watch it!" I growled.

"Sorry!" came the squeaky reply and I looked down to see one of my artists, James, who'd worked with me at my last job.

Reaching for him I mumbled, "Sorry! Sorry, dude, didn't see you. You okay?" softening my tone and rubbing James' shoulders. Seeing James nod quickly, his face red from embarrassment, I continued, "I gotta run. Appointment. And I'm late. I have my cell if anyone needs me and my tablet. It's unlikely I'll be back today."

"Oh, okay boss," the guy stammered.

Glancing at him quickly I realized with no small amount of guilt, that I'd knocked the iced coffee James had been holding and it had spilled down his shirt. "I'll pay for dry cleaning, just let me know how much. Sorry, I wasn't looking where I was going. I really gotta run. See you tomorrow?" Turning, I didn't wait to hear a reply and didn't look back at James who seemed frozen. *Shit! The gossips are gonna love this.*

***

The appointment had been at the gym, with a punching bag. Sometimes hitting something was the only way to get the anger out, to work out my aggression on the battered leather. It was something that had been recommended by a therapist during my teens after another expulsion. Yet I kinda felt that coming here had maybe been a mistake as the whole place was filled with memories of Andy. He'd been the one to introduce me to the place, and later offered to spot me while I lifted, when we happened to appear there at the same time. Feeling strangely nostalgic and thinking of him brought me back to my first day's meeting with the board and my new co-manager.

Parker PR and Advertising was supposed to be my fresh start. I didn't know anyone in this place so I couldn't be accused of getting the job through nepotism. The job was mine based on pure talent and ability. I'd earned this and I deserved it all on my own merit.

Somehow though, in my haste to take the job, I'd missed the part where the title was a joint one. There was already a project manager and he seemed well liked and respected, so it was unlikely he was shit at his job and about to be fired for me to replace him. Clearly, I'd frowned at my thoughts and the other guy must have seen it, thinking that the frown was for him. He glared back at me, which was just great, I thought to myself. Alienating a colleague in less than five minutes? A new record, I berated myself, internally rolling my eyes. Well, I wasn't there to be liked, and as long as this guy stuck to his lane, I would be cool and professional.

It turned out that I wasn't going to be working under Andy. Freddie had corrected that notion immediately seeing the tension that both of us held. Clearly someone was feeling a little threatened, I thought with an inner chuckle. I'd get to lead my own team and I would be instrumental in hiring them, with the board adamant that I chose people that I was comfortable working with rather than picking the people that they wanted me to hire. This had left me confused until I saw how differently things were run at Parker's on the brief tour that a prickly Andy took me on. Open plan work spaces, close knit teams, flexible working hours, working from home if they preferred, fruit and treats in the break room.

I'd been astounded when I'd learned that Parker's board had turned down clients with short deadlines, but attempted not to look too impressed, earning me an eye roll from Andy. They insisted that their *team not be overworked, had a work/life balance and that the people and companies they worked with operated ethically. My father would've had a conniption at all this "hippy dippy lark" as he'd have put it, rest his soul, in hell, where he deserved to be.*

All I knew was that it seemed to be working. The data on output was fantastic. Sickness was minimal and the quality of the work outstanding, with Parker's racking up a ton of industry awards. The people in the office looked so calm and settled. Staff turnover was nominal and this made me regret having not made the move months before when Parker Senior had come head-hunting me.

Not that I'd felt that straight away. Parker PR and Advertising had been something of a culture shock initially, especially with how rocky my relationship had been with Andy. Establishing a new team had been so stressful and time consuming that I'd thought about quitting. Then there were issues with Andy. We needled at each other often, personalities clashing I guess. Never anything big enough to need a visit to HR for mediation. We were big boys, after all. Freddie had taken a bit of an interest in me, which was cool, and he made great pains to smooth any ruffled feathers with Andy's team as they often jumped to his defense. More than once I'd caught Freddie explaining the different atmosphere I'd come from and reminding my co-workers that it'd taken time for them to get used to the changes too. It had rankled me quite a bit that my behavior apparently needed justifying, that I was the odd person out, but Freddie had come to be a good friend, so I brushed it off.

Alfred Parker Senior was an interesting man and had tried to hire me several times personally, which was more than a little unusual. He was adopting a "new life strategy", having had an epiphany as he lay recovering in a hospital bed from triple bypass surgery, following his massive heart attack during a board meeting. His fellow board members and friends had worked hard to save his life as they waited on the ambulance, with more than one facing therapy as they dealt with both the shock and their own mortality. It was amazing to be working for someone who inspired such affection and loyalty.

On returning to work, Parker Senior determined that things had to change, or else they were working for nothing. "Can't spend money when you're dead," he'd famously said. After some research on different business models, they'd found one that had worked for them, while Alfred "Freddie" Parker Junior came onto the board, giving his beloved dad a chance to step back and heal properly. I had to admit that I was jealous of their relationship and wished that my own father had seen his heart attack as the warning it was, like Parker Senior had, instead of working himself to death with no one left to miss him. Parker Senior was a great man, one that I couldn't help looking up to and Andy was one of his favorites, although he denied that with a laugh when Freddie poked fun at him, while I'd laughed. Parker Senior had a thing for saving waifs and strays.

Looking back at the start of things made me wonder, not for the first time, if perhaps I'd overreacted this weekend. That kind of thing, the way I'd treated Andy, was what I would've done before my time at Parker's. I had changed, hadn't I? My actions had been deplorable really. Andy may get under my skin and drive me out of my mind at times, but he deserved to be treated better than he'd been. My guilt prickled at me, I didn't like acting like a prick, that was my brother Alex's territory. There was just something about Andy that put me on the defensive constantly. Maybe we were too alike? Something to prove? Daddy issues? *Who knows,* maybe it was just that Andy reminded me of my past.

Realizing I'd stopped pounding on the bag and was just resting my head against it, I felt the pain in my hands register; the knuckles had split and were bleeding. I'd wrapped them thoroughly, as I'd been trained to, but I'd been punching for too long and had put too much force into each punch, as if each thump on the bag would somehow absolve some of this guilt I felt. I just didn't know what to do.

Perhaps Andy was right and we needed to stop things. God knew I didn't want a relationship. Been there. Done that. Got fucked up worse. No thank you. Still, Andy sparked something in me that I hadn't felt in so long and I felt strange knowing that our little game of tit for tat was at an end. It rankled that Andy'd been the one to call the shots on this. What if we tried to be friends? I didn't know if there was enough there between us for that but didn't want to go back to what we were before we hooked up. Did Andy like me enough to be my friend if an orgasm wasn't at the end of it? Could I put up with Andy, with his quirks and the way he irritated the shit out of me, to have him treat me with the same care and kindness I had seen him treat his other friends with and not want more? To have him look at me without that heat in his gaze across the gym floor?

So, I would never admit this to anyone, ever, but I hadn't even looked at another person since I had met Andy. Yes, I was an equal opportunity kinda lover - it was about the person, not the parts they had or how they expressed their identity, thank you very much. This had shockingly been one of the few things I'd not been at odds with my father about. "Fantastic PR", my father had actually commended me on being so open! I'd scoffed in my father's face and had received a firm rebuke. Father never raised a hand - words were much more cutting, after all - and left longer-ranging damage.

I grabbed my towel up and slung it around my shoulders after wiping the sweat off my face. Picking up some cleaner from one of the buckets dotted around the open plan space, I cleaned the bag thoroughly. Deciding to have a steam and see if that helped release some of the tension that'd settled along my wide shoulders and in my neck, I headed towards the back of the gym where the sauna and steam rooms were.

Dropping by the water fountain, I took a long drink in the hopes that this headache building was from dehydration and not a tension migraine, as I could be out of the office for days being unable to drive, and I had so much to do. Last time I had one, my output had dropped dramatically, being unable to bear looking at my tablet for any length of time, to the point that Andy had somehow heard I was ill and had visited me. The memory of that made me cringe when I thought of my behavior back then. I really was an asshole.

The phone rang on the console table by the door. It was the front desk security for the building asking if Andrew Barker was on the welcome list at my condo. At first I was confused. The pain was making grasping at thoughts like holding water in my hands, and processing anything was slow going.

Who was Andrew Barker? Then I remembered and gruffly allowed Andy to come up.

Tapping at the door came a few minutes later and I'd shuffled to the door, trying to avoid any sudden or jarring movements. Dressed in sweatpants and a faded black t-shirt from the day before, unshowered and bed-rumpled, I knew I looked far from my best.

I roughly jerked the door open, wincing as the sudden movement spiked pain through my head. "What do you want?" I demanded of Andy with a glare. A less than polite greeting, but I felt like shit and just needed to go hide in my darkened bedroom, not to be dealing with an unwanted visitor.

Andy looked startled at my gruff manner. While we constantly skirted the boundaries of rudeness at work, this was the first time we had seen each other outside of it.

"Um…" he cleared his throat, seemed to gather himself and said, "I heard you weren't feeling well from James," he seemed a little concerned. "Said something about horrendous tension migraines and um…" Andy seemed to stall at the glower I was sending him at this over share from James. Visibly straightening, he continued, "my mom got migraines a lot and she swore by this medication," showing me a package he fished out of his messenger bag, "and a bag of peas on the back of the neck, with your feet in warm water. Though that might not work for tension ones, so um, I could give your shoulders and neck a massage with this really good essential oil mix she swore by. I don't know what's in it, but Mom taught us to work the reflexology points too, if you'd rather not have a massage from me." Andy paused looking me straight in the eyes and all I could see was this

sweet earnest need to help. My skin prickled, gut churning with anxiety.

"Why?" was all I could bring myself to say.

"Look, work is work. We're competitive for the best jobs and you run your team how you like. There's no real need for us to be besties or anything, but getting along at work somewhat, would actually help. There may've been an email sent to both of us about our blow up last week." Andy winced as he said that last part with a look of shame, seeming to have taken the blame for letting it get out of hand. Stupid really since I had been in the wrong and was too embarrassed to admit it. Halfway through the argument I'd realized it but just couldn't back down.

"I didn't want to come," he blurted. "Parker Senior heard from Freddie that you were off and about our argument, so he got on my case a little about you and me. He wants us to get along. Basically, he said I should offer an olive branch, so here I am." The last part was said with a shrug. "You gonna let me in?"

Deciding to grab that olive branch, I stepped back from the doorway, allowing Andy into my spacious condo. "Nice place," said Andy appraisingly as he glanced about the place.

It wasn't nice. Sterile was the word I would use to describe it. Yes, the furniture was all new, sleek and white with a black leather sectional and black accessories, but it wasn't a home, it was cold. My mother had hired a decorator after I'd purchased the condo with my inheritance, insisting that it was time to move out of her home. Living with her had been an unavoidable necessity. Part of me *wondered if the decorator and all her help was a way to assuage her guilt over how things had turned out.*

"Freddie and Senior have a point but I feel like shit, man, and the last thing I want to do now is pander to anyone or play nice. I just want to take some more painkillers and sleep this off, which was what I was about to do before you turned up," I barked. Lies. I'd been on the couch feeling sorry for myself and debating on if I could get a food delivery person to pick up more painkillers while bringing me some food. When was the last time I ate last anyway? My stomach felt hollowed out.

Andy was starting to look irritated with my tone which gave me a sick sense of satisfaction. I wanted to get under Andy's skin as much as Andy got under mine. I wanted to poke and rile and fester there until Andy snapped. In the silence that followed my words, my stomach took the opportunity to growl its displeasure at the lack of food from the previous day. Clearly hearing it, Andy smirked. "Right, let's feed you, get this medication in you, and then I can get outta here and let you sulk or whatever. Then I can honestly say I visited and tried to help. Clear conscience," he smugly stated.

After almost force feeding me some toast and fluffy, perfectly scrambled eggs, Andy gave me the pills with a glass of water and perched on the coffee table. "Gimme your foot," he demanded. "I'm going to work on some pressure points like my mom showed me, then I'm outta here and we won't talk about this again."

I lifted my right foot and Andy grabbed at it, clasping it with both hands in his lap. His face was serious as he moved his long fingers over pressure points in my foot firmly, causing an indescribable feeling to rise in me. Before I knew it I could feel my dick getting hard and I squirmed on the sofa a little trying to discreetly adjust my cock in my sweats. Unfortunately Andy noticed my predicament, my gray sweatpants hid nothing. There was a reason they were used for thirst trap pics after all. His face flushed scarlet, "Mom never mentioned this happening with clients." he muttered.

"A reflex. There's been a dry spell. It isn't you, don't flatter yourself," I bit out with a sneer, feeling humiliated at my body's reaction to Andy's hands on me. Then the single worst thing I could've said followed, "Do you give happy endings like your mom did? That'd really release some tension." Silence echoed and Andy's mouth gaped before his face turned a furious shade of red. Dropping my foot like it was electrified, he got up, abandoned his things without a word, and left.

Three - Andy

It was Friday and the office was abuzz with gossip. Unfortunately, it was about me and Will. The speculation was that we'd both gone for a contract and Will was furious that I'd won it, which is why he hadn't been in the office since he stormed out on Tuesday.

There was even talk that Will was going to quit. James had heard that and had looked a little green before Freddie had found him and informed him that Will was ill and needed James to lead their current contracts. Obviously gossip was getting out of hand and needed to be nipped in the bud.

Clara was the gossip queen and my first point of call. "Hey Clara," I greeted the small brunette as I paused next to her desk. She was busy looking through samples and I hated to interrupt her, but I really didn't want another intervention from Parker Senior. While I loved the older man, he loved to meddle, especially when he saw something that needed fixing. If it got back to him that me and Will weren't talking again, there was sure to be another intervention.

I'd been in Will's apartment only once since I had visited during "the migraine incident" as he was calling it, one that had resulted in the only true apology from Will, ever. The second visit hadn't ended any better either, with me accidentally overstaying my welcome by sleeping the whole night after being fucked into the mattress by Will. This necessitated a brief but glorious shower the next morning to wash off the smell of cum. Will had been cold as he laid down rules post shower and I hadn't spoken to him for a week after that for talking to me like I was a child. I'd vowed never to return to Will's place after that morning's fight so there were no care packages in Will's future from me. Anyway, I was sure my presence would be unwelcome.

There was a part of me that felt that maybe Will's absence was because of me, a little squirming feeling of guilt. Perhaps it was my fault and Will was avoiding me but even that didn't feel quite right. Will had shown me, over and over, that we weren't anything, just a convenient hookup, so there was no way that there were feelings involved. He must truly just be feeling unwell. It wasn't the first time a migraine kept him out of the office either.

Clara looked up at me pushing her gold framed glasses up her nose. "Hey boss, what's up?"

"Nothing much, just getting James up to speed since Will's off with a migraine. I've had to take on some of their stuff to stop them falling behind, so I might need you to put in an hour or two of overtime next week, is that okay?" I asked her.

She gave me a quick smile. "Sure! You've had chickenpox, right?"

 "Ugh, yeah?" I looked at her, confused until I realized Suneya was missing. "Is Akio ill? Do you need time off too?" I asked, concerned about their little guy.

"Akio is fine aside from a good dose of chickenpox and nah," Clara interrupted. "Work is my quiet time away from the family. Suneya has this handled. We might switch out next week depending on how needy he is. He always prefers her when he's ill, which I get, she's far more patient than I am," she said with a laugh and I laughed with her as this was no lie.

31

Suneya was a saint for putting up with Clara at times; add in a four year old, and I had no idea why Suneya wasn't prematurely gray from stress. "Your wife is an angel," I said to her. "Take time off if you need it or do what I assume Suneya is doing, and work from home if you can manage."

"Thanks boss," she said, giving my hand a squeeze.

***

Later on I caught Clara filling in the interns and runners that Will was off ill and that between us, James and I had everything in hand. Sighing with relief at that bullet dodged, I took a minute to think about whether I should contact Will and check in with him. While we might not be hooking up any more, we still had to work together and we couldn't lose all the progress that we'd made in the interim of our...whatever we were calling it. Disaster is what Abigail referred to it as.

Thinking of my twin, I picked up my phone and asked her if she wanted to get dinner. As much as I liked my Friday gym sessions and drinks with the guys, I really didn't feel up to fielding their questions about Will. In fact, I thought that maybe it'd be better to catch one or two of them individually and ask them not to say anything. I knew we hadn't been very discreet at the gym, or at the bar, but I was hopeful that since Will had been friends with them too before he and I had started hooking up, that Will wouldn't want to cut them out just to avoid me. Sending off a quick text to Henry would be best. He was the ringleader and the most level-headed of the group.

Andy - Hey dude, no gym for me tonight or drinks. Am having dinner with Abby.

Henry - NP man, next week? Have you changed days? Haven't seen you or Will.

Andy - Yeah man, shit's been weird with him so been trying to give him some space. He's been off work sick, too. We aren't hanging out anymore.

Henry - REALLY? *shocked face emoji*

Andy - Seriously, it's a big thing *rolling eyes emoji* he didn't want you guys knowing we were hooking up.

Henry - *three laughing face emojis* dude he was not subtle about it. So you guys aren't together?

Andy - Nah, just scratching an itch on occasion.

Henry - Weekly, at least.

Andy - Whatever. Over now anyway. See you next week sometime?

Henry - How about coffee or a game over the weekend?

Andy - Sounds good, let me know what the plan is.

Henry had clearly been the right choice, though I was curious as to what the others would think about all the drama when they heard. It hurt to be so dismissive of the thing I had with Will, which is why I knew it was the right choice to stop. I scrubbed a hand through my artfully messy dirty blond hair, took a deep breath and pushed thoughts of Will away.

Four - Andy

As my twin, Abigail always felt that it was her responsibility to ensure "her little brother was happy". She only had ten minutes on me, but that was enough for her.

For the most part, it'd just been the two of us during our adolescence while mom worked two jobs to keep a roof over our heads after dad walked out on us, up until we lost her in an accident when we were in college. Abby had graduated with a costume design degree and worked the theater circuit with the occasional movie thrown in. Work wasn't always consistent so Abs also worked out of the home she shared with her boyfriend as a tailor. Alterations had partly funded college expenses and filled the fridge when we had lived with mom.

Dark to my light, with dark brown hair and chocolate-colored eyes. Smaller than me, but with a much bigger personality, my sister was fierce with a long memory when it came to people that hurt me.

Dylan Jeffries from third grade knew this well. So I really didn't want to tell her about what had happened with Will last week. Never having been a fan of the guy in the first place, this would forever keep him on her shit list. That list was long and getting off of it took some serious amount of work.

Giving her a dinner invitation soothed ruffled feathers. Avoiding Abby when she figured something was wrong wasn't an option. Some sort of twin sense must have activated on the weekend as she had been blowing up our chat all week before I'd relented and agreed to a face to face. I'd even tried inviting Josh to our dinner in the hopes that her boyfriend would be a buffer but he'd point blank refused, knowing that Abby was on a mission to work out what was wrong.

The restaurant that we met at was a firm favorite and reminded us both of the one that mom had worked at. Sometimes it was bitter-sweet, especially on the days that her loss was still fresh. Today though, I knew that our mom would be proud of what we'd achieved. College degrees, stable-ish jobs, homes and a loving relationship, in Abby's case. Josh literally worshiped the ground she walked on. Had since the first day they met in college. The only bone of contention was that Abby wouldn't marry him.

Expecting Abs to be late as usual, caught up in some project or other, I took our usual booth and ordered when the server approached. The buzz in my pocket made me smile, expecting a text from her to say that she was running late, or was on her way. Glancing at the screen I was surprised to see a text from Will, a reply to the one I had sent earlier in the day.

Andy - Just letting you know that between us, James and I have all your current projects up to date. Hope you feel better soon.

Will - Thanks, I appreciate that. Less to worry about for Monday.

Less to worry about? That was confusing, what did he mean? I sat, lost in thought about what Will had meant, until my sister plonked herself down in the booth opposite me.

"Hey you, sorry I'm late," she said, not looking very sorry at all. She looked a little harried, like I'd interrupted her, like this dinner hadn't been planned for most of the day.

"What're you working on?" I asked since my mind was drawing a blank on what was running in the theater that she usually worked at. Abigail was starting to get a name for herself, which made me very proud, knowing how talented she was and how hard she worked.

"Oh there's a new Shakespeare reworking planned, but they're taking the costuming in a different direction than you'd think. Kinda futuristic dystopian, with a lot of recycling of materials. It's weird but it's so fun coming up with concepts! This time they're going with a couple of my drawings!" Abby was practically vibrating out of her seat, excitement shining and I could only smile at her.

"I'm so proud of you, and mom is too, wherever she is, I'm sure of it," I told her. I could see her eyes fill up a little, but she pushed back the tears as the server approached to take her order.

Dinner went on as normal. We did this as often as schedules and budgets allowed, and often Josh tagged along. I really liked the guy, it was hard not to. Although he had been one of those jock types that smaller guys like me tried to avoid, he didn't fit that stereotype. Tall, dark and handsome, sure, but also smart, kind and devoted to my sister. Josh worked as an elementary school teacher, ran the after school homework club once a week, and also coached soccer.

For the majority of the meal it looked like she wasn't going to press, that Abby hadn't noticed that anything was off with me, but I must have been acting a little twitchy. We managed to get to dessert without her interrogating me. She must've been trying to lull me into a false sense of security because when she asked, "What's Will done now?" I broke straight away and told her everything over our slices of lemon cheesecake.

Seeing her frown, and knowing how concerned she was, made me feel awful. I knew if Josh was treating her the same way, I'd be livid, but there was just something about Will that had me putting up with it. Time and time again he sucked me back into our dysfunctional whatever, it certainly couldn't be called a relationship. Will was allergic to them.

"Look, this time it's really different. I've ended it. Made it absolutely clear. I can show you the messages if you want. He knows it too. We're done," I said firmly, while she gave me a gentle smile.

"Ew no, I don't want to see what you two send to each other." I let out a loud laugh that startled other diners, some turned to look at us. Abby let out a little giggle at my expression and covered her face while I went red with embarrassment. "Nah, Will didn't like to leave a trace of us being anything more than colleagues or even work out buddies," I muttered, wrinkling my nose a little with distaste. I really was fucked up for letting him get away with it for so long.

"Will you be okay?" She asked me. "I'm worried about you after last time."

I nodded at her, trying to look confident. I had to work with Will, I knew that getting into anything with him when we started could end up with me having to leave Parker's, but I did it anyway. I'd been there since straight out of college and worked my way up. It'd taken years of crazy hard work, long hours and crap pay. To risk all that for Will really said something. Somehow, I didn't think it would come to that. If things got too uncomfortable at work, I think Will would leave before I did.

Abby was intently studying me from across the table. The low hanging lights above us showed the reds and browns in her dark hair. Her brown eyes narrowed as she thought something through. Taking a breath, she started to say something and then stopped, clearly reconsidering.

"Okay," she started before she paused again. She gave her head a little shake and continued, "I think this really is it for you this time. I know you've said so before but there *is* something different about it this time. I think he really hurt you." Abs held up a hand as I went to interrupt her. "He did, don't deny it. You've always had more in this messed up whatever than he did and you should just admit that. You felt or maybe still feel something for him, but this weekend was the breaking point, or maybe you've just finally realized you are so worth more. Maybe now's the time to break your pattern. I think I should give you some dating help, since I'm clearly better at it than you."

This time I couldn't help chiming in, "Uh no, you and Josh were fate or some shit. It doesn't make you better than me at dating."

I gave her a smirk, but she fired back, "Yet, if you think back on all the guys you've dated, there are only one or two that weren't creeps or awful."

She paused for a second then continued as if I hadn't butted in to question her expertise, "So, I think that maybe in a few weeks, once you've had a little time, you'll be ready to move on and I have someone for you!" She looked a little giddy as she said the last part and I could only groan and put my head in my hands. Sensing I was about to say no, she cut in, "Not yet, obviously. Can't waste him on you if you aren't going to stop seeing Will. Jonas deserves better, but I think that you two would really hit it off." She really sounded smug now.

I raised my head and gave her a calculating look. "Jonas? As in Jonas Temper? From that sci-fi show that finished a little while ago?" Now she looked ready to gloat, knowing that I'd had a bit of a crush on him since I'd seen him in the show. Hell, I'd only stuck out the last abysmal season because of his character.

"That's the one," she practically sang. I was never going to live this down, she had me.

"So basically, you're in the position to set me up with my dream man, but are holding that over me until I do what you want?"

Her grin slipped with my words. My tone had meant to be teasing, but I think I was still too raw after admitting how bad things had gotten. How little self worth I apparently had. "Andy, no, it's not like that. I just don't want to set you up with someone, anyone, when you aren't ready to let Will go. You usually justify what he says and does," she started pleading with me, "I just want you to be happy and I don't think he's it for you. I'd go full on Stabby mode if you'd let me, but you won't." She pouted. "Give it a couple of weeks and then maybe you'll be ready for someone else. Maybe Jonas will be that someone." Abby looked upset that she had hurt my feelings, but I knew she was right. Meeting anyone right now would be a mistake because I wouldn't be able to give them a fair chance.

I looked her straight in the eyes as I said gently, "You're right. Now isn't the time." She gave me a smile and a laugh as I insisted she tell me everything about how she knew Jonas. Why he was in the city, and all about her new projects. We talked until late, ordering coffee after our generous cheesecake slices were demolished and only heading out when the servers asked us politely to leave. Josh was there to meet her and they took me home before taking off to their cozy place.

As I got ready to sleep, I kept my thoughts away from Will. When I got comfortable in bed, sleep didn't feel miles away as it had all week. *Nothing like having a hot guy as an incentive to stay on the right path,* I thought with a smile just as sleep took me.

Five - Will

Being stuck at home with a migraine had given me a ton of time to stew over my situation. When the message came in from Andy, I had to admit that I was both relieved and disappointed in equal measures. He seemed to truly mean that we were done. Inside, frustration still smoldered. I didn't want to have to let what we had go. It didn't make sense, but there was a part of me that'd loved the chase and when I'd gotten him, that part had changed to love the hold over him that I seemed to have. There was this sense of power over him and it'd been addictive. Clearly though, my actions had finally crossed the line after months of pushing at him, and I knew I would have to apologize for that, make sure that we would be cool working together. There was no doubt in my mind that if we couldn't at least be civil in the office that I would be the one to leave.

The one thing I knew with absolute certainty was that Parker's wouldn't be the same without Andy. The people there loved him. They tolerated me (well, except for Freddie), but we were only a couple of years apart and had moved in similar circles. He'd been aware of the fallout of the stuff with my brother and my ex, and had stayed out of my hiring so no one could question it. So Andy had to stay there. I could leave, and if it got really bad, I'd leave the city.

Moving was something to seriously consider. There wasn't much holding me here. My mom and my sister Matilda could visit wherever I went. Matilda was still picking colleges, being so much younger than the rest of us, so I could move to where she was headed. Only eighteen to my thirty-three, she was practically a baby still.

Alex was the eldest of us at thirty-five. Charlie, my youngest brother, had just turned thirty, and though mom had made sure I'd been invited to his lavish birthday bash, I'd declined. The only gift I'd be liable to give him would be a punch in his smug asshole face. The only people I hated more than Charlie were Alex and Helena.

With Andy texting me to let me know that my projects were in hand, the last of the tension I'd been holding finally slipped away. It was such a normal text and that gave me hope.

I didn't want to leave Parker's. I really loved my job and I liked the people there. I'd miss Freddie and James in particular. Andy too, in a weird way. So maybe we could just try and be friends. Sure, Andy didn't fit in my usual social circle, but neither did I any more. Not since all the drama with my brothers. Shrugging off those thoughts and finally feeling human for the first time this week, I considered my weekend.

Freddie had told me to take today off too when I spoke to him yesterday even though I assured him I could probably work from home. My tablet screen didn't have me wincing in pain any more. However it seemed I'd managed to accrue some overtime hours and was due the time back so he'd asked me just to relax and meet him for coffee on Monday.

Having a soak in the tub did nothing to ease the stiffness in my muscles and I thought about heading to the gym doing some stretching and having a steam. I wasn't quite fit for my usual workout and hadn't set foot in the place since Tuesday's boxing session. Scrolling through the app on my phone, I realized there were massages offered, including head and face, which would help with the lingering pain. With my day planned, I booked an appointment and started to get ready.

The gym was halfway between my condo and Andy's little apartment. Andy lived closer to work than I did and I had looked at places in the newer building next to his but my mother insisted the condo she chose was great value for money and was twice the size of the place we had looked at. Andy's place, while probably less than half the size of mine, was a home. It had a warmth that I found myself envying. I shrugged off thoughts of him, knowing that dwelling on the situation wasn't going to change anything.

The day was warm but with a heavy grey sky that threatened at least rain, perhaps a storm, so it was a blessing to enter the gym with its cool air-conditioned space. Holly, one of the owners, and her brother, Henry, were at the reception desk talking over something that they could see on the screen. Henry was a tall guy, muscular from all his private trainer sessions, with close cropped hair. I told him once that he reminded me of Idris Elba, though his skin was a lighter brown due to his and Holly's blonde mother.

Although Henry was a great looking man, I wasn't his type. At all. The guy was as straight as an arrow and had been with his girlfriend for a while now. His sister, Holly, had reminded me initially of Helena. The same take no shit attitude, beautiful and smart, but after flirting with me a couple of times she'd gotten the hint. I'd heard that she was dating someone and now that I knew her better, I hoped that this guy was worthy. Hearing my approach they both looked up, Holly with a friendly smile and Henry with a strangely blank expression.

"Hey," I greeted them both, "How's it going?"

Holly was the first to speak, "Oh hey Will, haven't seen you in a while. You in for a workout or do you need to book something?"

Since Henry was standing back and letting Holly deal with me, I turned a little and directed my words at her, "No workout for me, I overdid it the other day and my hands are still healing from the punching bag the other day, but I'm actually booked for a massage."

Holly looked down at the screen in front of her and clicked on a few things before laughing, "Oh! So you're my last-minute 3 o'clock. You picked up a cancellation. You're early though, and I was just gonna take a quick break first if that's okay with you?"

"Yeah of course, I thought about having a steam first if that's okay?"

"It is, just come on up to the first floor about ten minutes before your appointment, okay?" Holly gave me a smile before getting up and heading to the staff room, leaving me with a distinctly uncomfortable looking Henry.

Tension crackled between us and I realized that Andy had already spoken to him.

"Look," we both started to say before grinning at each other.

I went to start to speak again before Henry interrupted me, "Yes, I've spoken to Andy but I'm not here to take sides on whatever drama you two've going on. This is my family's gym and it's drama-free and I'm keeping it that way. You two are welcome here as long as you don't bring crap with you. The rest of the guys don't know stuff, but I can talk to them if you like so you don't have to. Both of you are our friends, but we won't take sides on it." He paused and then laughed, breaking the ice between us. "Honestly, I'm just glad not to have complaints about you fucking in the showers anymore." Henry laughed again and I couldn't help laughing along with him, even though I was embarrassed that he knew about that.

"Sure thing man, tell them whatever. It'll make it easier on both of us if we don't have to constantly go over stuff." I stopped, running a hand over the back of my neck feeling a little sheepish, not having talked to anyone about Andy before. "We were hooking up, but nothing more."

I blew out a breath. "Andy wants space and I'll give him that." My tone was resigned. "Maybe down the line a bit we can be friends, I don't want it to be weird." I caught a glimpse of skepticism crossing Henry's face when I said that Andy wasn't more to me than a hookup, but I didn't have the energy to set him straight. Maybe I'd come across as a little defensive. There was still a lot of shame deep inside over how I'd overreacted.

After catching up with Henry and missing my steam altogether, I went upstairs for my massage with Holly feeling that things with Henry and the other guys would be fine. Now, I just had to get there with Andy.

Six - Andy

The alarm on my phone blared from the night stand and I stretched before shutting it off. Laying in bed, I took stock of how I was feeling about the day ahead. Will would be back in the office today and I had absolutely no idea how that was going to go. Instead of freaking out about it though, I'd settled into a weird calm.

Saturday had been stormy all day, so instead of a soccer game with the guys, we'd gone out to dinner at a great but cheap pizza place a few blocks from the gym that Henry and his sister owned. Henry had pulled me aside to let me know that all Will discussions were off the table and he and the guys were now declared Switzerland. I'd laughed at Henry's Twilight reference before thanking him. It was great to go out with the guys and blow off some steam, to try and get my thoughts off of Will for a bit.

While brushing my teeth after my shower, I caught myself reaching for my prescription of PrEP. It was a recently developed habit to take it first thing, unfortunately it was also reminding me why I'd started on it in the first place. Will. We'd been hooking up constantly for nearly two months when it happened.

Will suddenly stopped his desperate furious thrusting in and out of me with a sharp inhalation and a "fuck!!" He groaned against my neck as he reached his climax. I turned my head to look at him with difficulty from where I was, face against the wall.

As soon as we had gotten in my apartment he'd been on me, pushing me against the wall, kissing me like he hadn't been with me in weeks. Before turning me to face the wall, he pulled my pants down to my ankles and rimmed me until I'd begged him to fuck me. There wasn't much need for foreplay after our shower together at the gym, where we had nearly gotten caught. Again. He probably would have fucked me there if he'd thought to take a condom with him when he invaded my shower. I winced as he pulled out, feeling more than a little sore, I'd be feeling that for days. It was then that I felt a trickle of wetness run down my thigh.

"Shit!" Will exclaimed.

"What's wrong?" I wasn't able to connect the dots properly, more than a little cum drunk. My orgasm had hit me like a ton of bricks, some hitting the wall. I was too out of it to worry about it leaving a stain.

"The condom broke."

Will sounded horrified and I sobered immediately. "Did you cum? Is that what I'm feeling?"

"Yeah, I dunno what happened." I turned to see him putting his finger through the hole in the ruined condom.

"We were going a little rough, and maybe a little too dry?" I said softly, as he pulled on his boxers and perched on the arm of the sofa.

"Is it a problem? What's your status? I haven't been with anyone apart from you since my last test and I was negative. Nothing to worry about on my side." I rushed to get out, babbling in my desperate haste to soothe him as I simultaneously pulled myself

together, pulling up my pants and throwing back on my t-shirt from where it had landed on the floor.

He looked ready to bolt and we needed to discuss this. We were adults and we could act like ones, right? Will looked over at me and let out a breath. From where I stood, I could see his relief.

The adrenaline drop had me starting to shake. I needed to get cleaned up, have a drink and sit down or I was going to collapse. Leaning back a little, my legs stopped shaking as I was propped up by the wall. "Same here, nothing to worry about. No one but you since my last test either and I'm on PrEP." He paused, considering something. "Maybe, if you think, we could stop using condoms? That is, unless you plan on hooking up with someone else." He looked hesitant and this was a rare show of vulnerability from him. There was a tiny sliver of anger there too, that the idea of me with someone else got him riled up. "I'm not seeing anyone else and even though this is just a hookup, I don't want you with anyone else. I know that's selfish and wrong of me since I can't give you a proper relationship. I won't share you. Just you and me. Do you want that?"

I gave him a nod and he continued. "Eventually you might want more than what we're doing, but we can cross that bridge when we come to it. Y' know I don't want a boyfriend right now, what we have works and is as much as I can do."

I stopped him by saying firmly, "If I decide I want more and you still can't give me that, then we end things. In the meantime, I'm not going to sleep with anyone else, so yeah, I trust you and we can go bare. I've never done that before."

*He looked surprised for a second before he nodded.
"Maybe you should start PrEP, too?"*

*I thought about it for a minute and smiled at him.
"I'll call my doctor next week." He came over to me,
kissing me gently and helping me re-dress.
Checking I was okay one final time, he left.*

I took the pill, swallowed it without any water and
went to rustle up some breakfast. While I wasn't
planning on having sex with anyone for a while, it
was something less to think about and it was so
routine now for me to take it, so I'd just carry on
with it.

For the first time in a long time I felt calm and in
control. While Will's "less to worry about" comment
had been on my mind a lot over the weekend, I'd
decided not to dwell on it. I was confident that we
could keep it professional at work and maybe in a
couple of weeks I'd be ready for that date my sister
wanted to set me up on. I groaned just thinking
about how pathetic my love life had gotten that
Abigail had taken to looking for guys for me. While I
was grateful for her support, I couldn't help but
compare myself to her and it made me feel like shit.

***

If anyone in the office noticed anything off between
Will and I, they weren't saying anything. Truth be
told, we were probably acting better than normal.
There was none of the usual baiting or little digs.
Just careful, bland politeness.

Frustratingly, I missed how we'd been before. Now
I was being treated like nothing more than a
stranger. The guy had fucked me for months,
couldn't keep his hands off me whenever we found
ourselves alone, and now I was being treated like it

hadn't happened. It was actually starting to piss me off. In truth, it hurt more than it made me angry.

I hadn't started things with Will. Sure he was hot and all, everything about him ticked off that imaginary list, but I'd been determined that my crush on him wouldn't come to anything. No way was I going to make a move on him. The sexual tension between us had waned after the migraine incident, which I still hadn't told Abby about. She didn't need to hear how Will had insulted our dead mom. I'd been too angry to speak to him for days until he'd finally cornered me and begged for forgiveness.

It wasn't even that I thought her selling her services like that was morally wrong, you gotta do what you gotta do so you could eat. Her memory was precious and he'd tainted it by insinuating that. He'd apologized but it had taken us a while to get back to the status quo. After a couple of weeks, late into his second month at Parker's, things had eased between us, mostly because I couldn't hold a grudge. Will had seemed sincerely sorry, so I let it go.

We'd just finished up a test collaborative project. I call it a test as it was pretty low stakes. While it was a big enough task that it required both teams, we'd done work for this company before so we weren't treading new ground.

There had been doubts we could successfully pull it off, as our clashes were pretty regular at that time. Tame really, just insults, constant jabs and questioning, butting heads at almost every opportunity. The bump of the migraine incident was behind us and we'd found new common ground. However, the office didn't know that Will and I had called a truce and I'd just introduced him to Farmer's Fitness, Henry's gym.

I'd found the place about six months before while I was getting over a particularly bad break-up. My self worth had been next to nil and apparently, according to Jason, the ex in question, I'd put on a few pounds, but not in a cute way. Dick. So I'd been going to the gym for a bit, and gotten into great shape. In a meeting with Freddie and Will, Farmer's came into conversation and I'd ended up offering to meet Will there. He'd joined up that day.

The project meeting had finally wrapped up. As was the norm for us, we were the last people in the office, having assured our teams that it was okay to leave and there would be no destruction come morning. We were in the conference room gathering up materials, occasionally brushing against the other in passing, tension building with every seemingly innocent graze.

There had been small touches all day. Will had sat closer to me than was strictly necessary and more than once I'd been so distracted by him that someone had to repeat what they'd said. The feel of his thigh against mine, that small bit of contact had me questioning what was happening. More than once I thought I'd felt him sweep his hand along the inside seam of my leg, just a ghost of a feeling. To gain my attention he had put his hand along my arm adding a tiny, unnoticeable caress. When trying to discuss something privately, he'd turned his head and leaned into me so close that I felt his breath on my ear. I'd spent the entire day in a state of confused arousal.

I was taking cups to the break room, walking behind Will, when he turned suddenly and took the tray from me, setting it down on the counter. He just stood and looked at me for a minute. Awareness of how close we were standing prickled along my skin and my breathing picked up. Seeing my reaction, his eyes darkened and a smirk lit his face.

I swallowed, mouth dry, and Will's eyes tracked the movement. He reached a hand, grabbing up my tie and pulling me towards him. He leaned down, his words brushing against my lips, "You want this, don't you?" He moved forward so that our lower bodies touched. I felt the length of him hard against my stomach, my equally solid dick against his thigh. It was painful after being hard half the day.

I gasped as I felt him. "Yes," I had managed to get out and without hesitation, he leaned down the last inch between us and claimed my mouth. Just took complete ownership of me and I was happy to let him.

Now I'd had great first kisses before, but this was a kiss to redefine all kisses. As his tongue licked into my mouth he used the hand grasping my tie to pull me closer into him, until there was no space between us. Melting into him, I gave into it and my hands started to explore.

First his lower back, pushing my hands up the broad expanse to his shoulders, bunching his charcoal shirt in my fists as I clutched him tightly, my tongue twined with his. Then my hands moved of their own accord, up along his neck before they found their way into his hair. I desperately pulled at the dark strands, wanting to keep his lips on mine forever. He groaned as my fingers tightened and I could only moan in response. His hand left my tie to hold my chin, cupping my throat, dominating me completely. His kiss became more demanding, forceful as if he wanted to own me, and his other hand fell to my ass, holding me firmly against him.

We broke apart briefly to breathe before our lips touched again and clashed.

Some time later I became aware of the noises of the cleaning crew arriving outside and reluctantly pulled away from him. He looked down at me, hands cupping my jaw and thumbs brushing along my cheekbones before planting a simple, sweet kiss on my swollen and bruised lips.

"Hmm, you taste so damn good. Addictive. I want to keep going, but not here." His voice held a delicious raspy quality. Another kiss was pushed onto my lips before he stepped back to a more appropriate distance. And I knew right then that if we went home together it would be the hottest night I'd ever have. But it would only be one night because while I didn't know much about him, I knew he was a one and done person, and that wasn't me.

"I don't think that's a good idea," I said, struggling to get the words out. His expression flashed with disappointment before it shuttered. There was nothing left in his expression to help me guess what he was feeling. It was just a beautiful, but blank, face. He went to ask something, but the sounds drew closer and we were interrupted before he could get the words out. I caught him looking at me as I greeted the cleaners I knew, then he just walked away.

Seven - Andy

Half the week had passed quickly, as I'd thrown myself into any project going and Will had a few things to wrap up with the project I'd assisted them on. Things had thawed marginally between us since Monday, but we were still far from our usual selves.

I tried to push away the hurt, especially since I'd been the one to end things, but I knew deep down that it'd been an excuse since I'd caught feelings for Will. He'd treated me poorly, sure, but it wasn't the only reason for stopping the sex with Will. He'd been a bastard to me more than once and I'd continued to have sex with him after he had grovelled a bit.

A part of me wanted him to beg me not to end it, to show that he felt something for me in return. I guess that's why I was hurting so badly, because after that initial storming out of the office where he had been "fine," there was nothing coming from him that made me feel like I was anything more than a convenient hole when the need struck him, and that just stung like a motherfucker. I'd thrown myself a pity party in an attempt to get it out of my system, but knew it would take more than that.

So, I was still hung-up on the guy. He was different from most of the guys that I'd been with before. More intense in a lot of ways, but he seemed to respect me, and would check in to make sure I was okay with everything we did. While he may have been a dick to me on occasion, he never took it too far, always knew when to apologize, mostly without actually saying sorry, as was his way. Our chemistry was insane. Together we just sparked and made the other better.

He ticked all my boxes, gorgeous with those soulful dark eyes and Grecian features from his late father. Tall and well-built, favoring boxing and martial arts over weightlifting, and oh so smart. We could bounce ideas off of each other at work and it was effortless. We could be great together. I just couldn't get why he couldn't see it and didn't want more than just a random stream of encounters. The danger of getting caught often took away from any pleasure and it wasn't like there was a policy at work forbidding relationships. Suneya and Clara were married for heaven's sake! To each other!

I blew out a breath and rolled my eyes at myself. "Idiot," I scolded myself aloud and got back to cleaning up my kitchen from the mess of the cookies I'd made. Going all out, I'd made triple chocolate chip cookies for the support group I was a part of.

The older volunteers helped with snacks on a roster for the kids and teens that we saw weekly. With limited access the the space, we alternated between Wednesday's and Thursday's with another group. Frustrating, but a lack of funding didn't give us much options. As I usually did when it was my turn to bring something, I made something home-made, believing that these kids deserved that extra bit of effort. They were grieving and needed to know they were worth that work.

I worked half the day at home in order to have the time, making calls while batches were in the oven. After the sessions, I would work out any lingering pain or sadness at the gym. I'd have to find another outlet today unless there was a late class. Brushing off that idea, I got myself ready to head out for the support group.

***

On Thursday, things had been pretty normal, until we were summoned to the conference room for a meeting and both teams had been asked to attend. Thankfully it wasn't my week for snacks at the support group but I let the others know I wouldn't be there in case the meeting ran over. I hated to miss out but it wasn't often that we were called to mandatory meetings like this.

It was unusual to only have the two smaller teams, but Parker's had undergone downsizing and restructuring together. They'd even moved buildings to get the right ambiance, trying a European style of working to see if that fit their new way of running the business. The whole project had added a level of prestige to the company that we'd never had before.

Freddie was running the meeting, not something that he often did, and he had a different energy than normal. Freddie was laid back and charming, but today he was buzzed and seemed a little frantic. I caught myself looking for Will to see if he knew what was going on and watched as he pulled Freddie into the corner of the room as things were set up. The two of them talked in low voices with Will laying a hand on Freddie's shoulder as if to reassure the older man.

Both Suneya and Clara were out of office today with their ill son having kept them awake most of the night before. Clara had managed a video call so I set up the tablet facing where Freddie would be sitting at an empty seat next to me with Jenny on my other side.

There was tension buzzing around the large room; everyone was picking up on the weird vibe. The AC was on the fritz so everyone was restless as the temperature climbed with us all stuffed in the overly warm room. At one point, I feared that Jen was going to pass out, so I got up to open some of the windows. I'd struggled with the latches before Will had come to assist me. Giving him a quick "thanks," I'd received a genuine smile in return. That little smile had eased something in me that I hadn't known needed to be soothed.

It took a while for the meeting to get going and more than once, Will jumped in to clarify a point. The long and short of it being that now that we had both managed to wrap up our respective projects for the most part, we were going to have to work together for a really big client.

There was a moment of silence as the room looked to me and then to Will. He'd obviously had a little bit longer to get used to the idea because he was calm as he said, "That won't be a problem."

I needed to wrap my head around it a little bit longer before I could get any words out and I just managed to keep an even expression on my face as I assured Freddie that Will and I could work together with no issues. Inside I wasn't as convinced, especially with being given the lead on it over Will. This could make or break us. Our first collaboration had set us on this path after all. If we couldn't do this, then one of us would have to leave.

When I got Will's text, I was nervous, and a whole swarm of butterflies took off in my stomach. Of course it was just my luck that everyone wanted to speak to me after the meeting broke up. Clara and Suneya gave apologies for not being here in person, or on the call in Suneya's case. I even got a glimpse of Akio, who was absolutely covered in chicken pox and looked utterly miserable. I did not envy them. At all.

Freddie came next with assurances that I was ready to take the lead on something of this size. Jenny had questions and I just felt unprepared and ready to burst from the stress of trying to pretend everything was fine.

What was Will going to say? Would he suggest that one of us leave? I couldn't imagine working anywhere else, as sad as that sounded. Parker's was family to me. Hell, Parker Senior had been in my life nearly as long as my dad had been. I certainly knew him better. Kinda tragic, really.

The selfish part of me didn't want to part with what had become a rather cushy job. I knew how others had it in the same industry and compared to them, I was pampered. The first couple of years here had been hard with long hours, few benefits, and a whole lot of stress. Straight out of school into the realities of a cut-throat industry had been an eye opener for sure. There had been a time when I thought I'd burn out.

I'd interned here during the summer before graduation and Parker Senior had taken a liking to me for whatever reason. The feeling had been mutual. He'd sat in on my interview as I was getting ready to graduate and I'm sure he was the reason that I got the job. I'd never had such great luck before and had fully expected to wait tables or work in a bar until I could get somewhere to take me on.

The thing was, I didn't want Will to leave either. He'd brought out something in my work that I hadn't expected. He had a different style that the company needed. He made us better. Made me work smarter. I felt more creative with him around.

Eight - Will

I owed Freddie one for giving me a heads up about this new project. Honestly, the guy could have anything he wanted, as it helped me save face in the meeting and in front of my team as I outlined what was expected of us.

Just two weeks ago, I would've been furious that Andy had been given seniority over me. I was older than him, but because I had worked for my father in finance for a couple of years, our experience in advertising was about the same. However, Andy had stayed through the restructuring and had been with Parker's for a long time, around seven years, so he knew how they operated better than anyone.

Deep down, I knew he deserved it. This last week had clearly given me a chance to be more objective about where we stood at work, if nothing else. Andy was also more of a people person than I was. I found it harder than he seemed to when trying to convince a client that a particular strategy was the way to go. He had this charm about him, and as corny as it sounded, a sort of inner light that drew people to him like moths to a flame or whatever.

I rolled my eyes internally at where my thoughts were headed. This guy had me so messed up. After trying for months to keep him at a distance, trying to have my cake and eat it (yes, I was using all the cliché sayings today), I could admit there were some feelings there. I just didn't know if I had it in me to do anything with them. Inside I was terrified about letting someone in. What we had was safe, easy, and fun.

On the outside, Andy didn't look like he would be as wild as he was. There was a mischievous streak to him that got my motor running. Sexually, our connection was intense, like nothing I'd felt before. Andy was sweet and kind. He needed to be kept away from all my bullshit.

Deciding that it was time to clear the air with Andy, I sent him a quick text.

Will: Could we talk after the rest clear out?

Andy: Sure, that's probably a good idea.

It was a relief to see that we were on the same page about this. Both of our futures at Parker's rested on this project going well. My plan was to let him know that I'd leave if we couldn't get our shit together. With plenty of money left over from my inheritance, and if I sold my apartment, I could start over anywhere and there'd be no rush to get a new job. There'd be time to figure things out.

The more I thought about moving, the more it appealed to me. Starting fresh. I also wondered if it was a knee-jerk response to the stuff with Andy; embarrassment around how we had ended our thing making me want to run away like a little kid.

Over the weekend I'd chatted with my sister about colleges and she had narrowed it down some. I'd kept the idea of following her quiet though, as I'd gotten the distinct impression that she was keen to strike out on her own, well away from our family and all the drama that came with it. Couldn't say that I blamed her there.

The room cleared out slowly and I could see Andy making excuses to hang back, clearly not wanting to let people know he was waiting for me. I turned to the materials in front of me and picked up my tablet, pretending that I didn't notice him.

One thing I'd learned early on was that Parker's loved gossip, and Clara was the gossip queen. Honestly, how Andy and I had kept our hook-ups under wraps baffled me. I didn't think that we were particularly subtle about some of the looks we had given each other, or that couple of times we had ended up in the bathroom together. Or that one time, in this conference room, where Andy had sucked me off from under this very table. My lips quirked as I remembered that.

It'd been a dare really, but he figured I'd thought he wouldn't do it. Often at the start of a week we would have other stuff going on so we didn't have the chance to meet up for sex. So, by the middle of the week, sexual tension was high.

Monday to Wednesday was foreplay for us. More so if I'd pissed Andy off, which, let's face it, was all too often. I'd flirt and tease to get back into his good graces, which didn't take all that much most of the time; it was more banter than really being angry with me. When he was really upset, I took those times seriously, because, despite how I'm sure it came across, I did care about him. One time, I actually sent him flowers here at the office to say sorry and his team had teased him about his "secret admirer" for days after. He instantly knew it was me when I winked at him.

After work he'd all but dragged me home with him, and shown his appreciation by sucking me off before I'd fucked him. We ordered take out and ate it in his bed before going another round. As he lay sleeping, I had lain awake, hesitating.

There was a part of me, one that had been growing, that wanted to wrap him in my arms and stay there all night, but the fear was still there. I wasn't ready

to risk my heart on more. So I tidied up, left a
cheeky note, and left him to sleep alone.

Andy's approach startled me from my thoughts, and
a grin quickly moved over his all too expressive
face. Andy was cute, and far too good for me. I
honestly didn't get why more guys weren't getting in
line to be with him.

His blond brown hair was cut close on the sides but
longer on the top, and after hours of the meeting, it
was messy from running his hands through it, often
in exasperation. He loved it when I ran my fingers
through his hair, grabbed at it and pulled, no more
so than when he had my cock in his mouth. He'd
wink and say, "harder" in that adorable way that got
me hot.

His big blue eyes reminded me of summer skies.
He hated that his nose was a little upturned and
had complained about it more than once, but I
loved it. I wanted to lay kisses on it. Andy's nose
gave his face character along with his thick brows,
full lips and sharp cheekbones. While he went to
the gym, he insisted it was to keep lean, and not for
any vanity. To me, he was perfection. He didn't
have a lot of body hair, and struggled to grow a
beard, but his skin was gorgeous, pale, smooth,
and soft. I'd never met anyone that I wanted more
with, ever. And yet I had to give him up because as
much as I craved him, he wanted more than I could
give. Deciding then and there that he needed to be
in my life somehow, I resolved to at least be his
friend. I could do that, right?

It was easy to see that he understood how
important this was just from the expression on his
face and the tentative way that he took a seat
opposite me. I frowned at the fact that he was all

the way over there. He wasn't afraid of me, was he? Had I really been that rough that I'd scared him?

That thought settled like lead in my stomach and bile rose in my throat. Rough play, when safe and consensual, was hot as hell. I was totally into that and, from experience, so was Andy, but the last time had been different in some way, more raw. I'd poured my stress and frustration into every thrust. Held a little tighter as I felt us slipping away from my careful control. Had I crossed a line? Any sort of abuse wasn't acceptable to me, and I needed to know for sure that I hadn't gone beyond his limits. There's no way I'd ever forgive myself if I'd scared Andy or caused him physical pain.

"I'm sorry," I blurted as he settled into the seat. "if I was too rough. The last time. I know I took it a bit too far, so if I…."

Andy smiled, and that more than anything made relief wash through me. "Nah, well, yes. Rougher than usual, but I know that if I'd asked you to ease up you would've. If I'd said stop you'd have stopped. You would've, right?" I nodded at him, beyond words at how grateful I was that I hadn't done irreparable damage to our relationship, thing, whatever it was.

Seeing that I was working through my thoughts, Andy forged ahead. "So we need to work together, but I think stopping the sex was probably the best idea. Even without last time, I think, if I'm honest…" his words came to a halt as his face flushed scarlet. Taking a deep breath, he went on, "It was starting to mean more to me than I think it was to you. I was wanting more. Dates, being around friends and family. No sneaking about. A proper relationship. You've been honest with me from the start that you don't want a boyfriend and I agreed to that, so, yeah..." he trailed off, clearly embarrassed at admitting all that.

A part of me just wanted to shout out, "I want all that! I want to be your boyfriend!" but fear kept me silent, and Andy took that to mean that he'd been right, that I didn't want a relationship still. I was so torn up about it. I could see what a real relationship with Andy would be like, and it looked like a dream. Friends, family, things I'd given up. To keep him in my life, I had to give him something and that dream was the cost.

"I'm not ready for that kind of thing and I don't know if I ever will be. I've had all that before and it was ripped away from me in the worst way." The words tangled up on my tongue, bitterness still fresh enough to choke me all these years later. "The pain that it caused changed me. But we have this project, the office, our friends at the gym...so we need to do something." Looking over at him, I smirked. "You've been avoiding places you think I might be." He looked ready to interject, so I held up a hand, "Henry told me about the different classes you tried." I laughed then remembering the story of the yoga class and the description of Andy's face as he iced his groin.

"What?" Andy looked horrified.

"Yoga."

He buried his head in his hands and groaned. "I'm gonna kill him. He said he wouldn't tell anyone!"

Laughter burst from me. "You didn't believe him, did you? You should know him better than that!"

Andy looked up at me with a mock glare before laughing too. "Fair point."

We took a minute, just enjoying being together without all the tension that had followed us lately. The last couple of weeks had been hard, and I think that I'd forgotten how much I liked being around Andy. "I think we should hang out, try and be friends, just friends, no benefits," I said with a wink and he gave a snorting laugh.

"Sounds like a plan to me. I'm in."

Nine - Andy

After clearing the air and finishing up at work, I was reluctant to go home. Seemed that my new "friend" had the same thought, as a text buzzed in my pocket.

Will: Gym? Been a while and it'd make Henry get off my case lol

Andy: Sounds like a plan. 7:30? I'm starving and need to get my stuff

Will: My gym gear is in my car. Wanna get something to eat first? We can swing by your place and pick up whatever you need

Was it too much too soon to be going out for food with Will? I shrugged that thought off. If we started off with me saying no, then we weren't going to get far at all. Truth be told, the idea of going home and eating alone wasn't very appealing. I wanted to see the guys. They might not be there, but Henry usually worked on a Thursday evening.

The other classes hadn't been working out for me, even without mild groin strain. I'd even tried Zumba and was bruised from it. Obviously, I was NOT coordinated enough for that one. The ladies of the class had been lovely, though. There was even the offer of being set up with sons and nephews, which Abby found hilarious.

Andy: I'm in. Dinner sounds good. I have my car though, so I'll go grab my gym stuff first. Meet at the restaurant?

Will: Meet you at Trixie's? Half an hour?

Andy: *thumbs up emoji*

***

Any worries that I may have had about it being strained or weird between us rapidly fell away as Will greeted me at the doors of Trixie's, a diner similar to the one that I often met Abby at. We were seated and had our orders taken quickly, both of us opting for sandwiches and salads rather than anything too heavy before our workout.

Conversation was easy and flowed, so much so that I'd to remind myself that this wasn't a date. We chatted about the office, projects and stupid little things. Deep down I knew it would take time for Will to truly become my friend, and that I'd have to keep emotional distance. It was this or nothing.

My heart nearly stopped when Will said, "I was planning on leaving Parker's if you didn't think we could work together." He looked sheepish. "Once you're done with someone, there doesn't seem to be a way back, so if you were done with me.....well, I think leaving would have been the best idea."

Sitting, likely gaping at Will, I looked for the words to assure him that I'd have made it work, but he shook his head at me, half-heartedly shrugging his shoulders. "Nah, honestly, I got the idea about moving into my head, and I think if we couldn't make it work then that would've given me an excuse, you know?"

I could only shrug, because even when things were pretty bad and I feared for my safety from my ex, Jason, I never thought about leaving. I dunno what that made me. Probably an idiot, like Jason had said.

"This is good though," I said after a pause, finally finding my voice. "It might actually make things better at work if we're on the same page, if we can find more common ground." He looked hopeful so I continued, "Even when I was really angry at you, I didn't think about cutting you out of my life. I just needed time to adjust back to what we were before. Honestly, Parker's wouldn't be the same without you." I gave him a genuine smile.

Gratitude lined his face and my heart's frantic beat eased. There was something about this softer, more open version of Will that was captivating. I wanted to hear all his stories, learn what made him smile, have him trust me with his secrets. Being his friend was going to have to be enough.

***

We walked to the gym from Trixie's, having left our cars at our apartments. The night was crisp and cool, with the trees that lined the sidewalks starting to show their gorgeous fall colors. In another few weeks, they'd begin shedding their leaves. It was almost fully dark, but it was impossible to see stars with the lights of the city obscuring them.

To begin with, we were silent, just enjoying the walk and the ease between us, but it wasn't long before we fell into that relaxed banter we had shared during dinner and some of our more memorable hookups. If all nights were as chilled as this, then pushing Will into the dreaded friend zone would be simple. Right?

When we walked into the gym, a huge two-story building converted from an old warehouse, it took a minute to adjust to the bright lighting. The ground floor had kept the oversize doors and hardwood floors, though in the equipment areas they were covered with black and navy thick mats that often muffled the sounds of weights hitting them.

Windows on the ground floor were the reflective kind, with the people inside being able to see us in the street while we couldn't see in.

The barn style doors slid open as we approached, Will jokingly shoving me to go in ahead. I thought that Henry was going to keel over in shock when he glanced up from his computer as we drew near. Laughter burst from me at his expression which Will quickly noted, his own booming laugh joining mine.

Henry scowled at us. "Laugh it up, fellas. We all thought we'd never see you two in the same place ever again. Pete has fifty on it taking a month. Looks like he lost that bet."

Will chuckled and I poked him in the ribs. "This one was missing me and we made up."

"Hardly," Will countered, his voice dry with the hint of a smile playing at his lips. "It just got too quiet, y'know?"

We fell quiet and the air filled with tension, the ease from outside gone. It was always so straight forward with just the two of us. Being around other people meant having to hide and lie. Henry's glances and grins to the others on that Friday night was the beginning of the end of our arrangement. Standing with us now, he acted as a reminder of why things had to stop. It sat heavy between us for a minute.

As strange as it was, Will and I didn't really hang out between hookups, not as friends. When we were with the guys it was more like colleagues or acquaintances. More often than not, we didn't even sit near each other if we went out with them to the bar. It acted as another layer of foreplay.

We'd thought we were being subtle, which was stupid because Henry had probably guessed we were the guys in the shower that someone else had reported having sex. He'd clearly been onto us for a while. Maybe he'd caught the loaded glances and the way Will would brush a finger along the back of my neck to tease me when he walked by. Or how we'd leave within ten minutes of the other leaving, one of us waiting outside or in another bar down the street.

"So....?" Henry started to ask the question I'd been dreading before Will cut in saying firmly, "We're friends and co-workers. That's it."

Not gonna lie, the last bit hurt and was going to keep on hurting until I could purge all these feelings I had.

Ten - Andy

A week passed by, and although we texted a fair bit, we hadn't made plans to hang out again outside of our usual workouts, which was fine I guessed. Never having been in this situation before, I didn't know how to navigate what was essentially being friends with an ex. Either my former exes dumped me in spectacular fashion, or I had to get a restraining order and a new cell number.

Unfortunately, that was no exaggeration. Jason was still under his restraining order eighteen months on. I'd moved after Dylan, another ex a couple of boyfriends before Jason, to my current place to escape him and he was banned from Parker's before he finally gave up.

Jason was the reason that Josh and Abby had lived in my apartment for a month, with me living at their place and working remotely. We'd pretended that I'd sublet the place to them and moved, not being able to afford to break my lease and unwilling to lose my apartment. Jason, thankfully, hadn't met my sister and I didn't have any recent photos of her on display, so he didn't realize we were related.

The commute from their house had been a bitch and so expensive. I'd only done it a couple of times before Jason caught me just outside of work and left me afraid to leave Abigail's for a week. It took that long for the bruises to go down, and for me to stop feeling ashamed that I hadn't defended myself better. Once the order was in place and he stopped appearing at my work, I'd returned home and changed as many things that I could afford to do, just so that it felt like my safe haven again.

That was part of why I was finding it so difficult to adapt to friendship with Will. First off, I wanted more than that. Second, I'd never done it before, it was a complete unknown. Will knew where the line was. Would make amends if he needed to and always meant it. If I said I was uncomfortable with something, he would stop. When I asked for space, I got it. Will respected me in a way that no other guy had.

The thing was, that respect had to go both ways. I couldn't push him into something he said he didn't want. I'd been given an explanation, however brief and lacking, that he wasn't ready, might never be ready, and I had to respect that. I wanted more, he didn't. Will had offered his friendship instead, and that would have to do.

***

Though Will and I hadn't hung out, our usual Friday hangout with the guys was back on. A shorter gym session, and then a few beers and some nachos at the bar down the street from the gym.

Will received a hug from Brad, his usual sparring partner, and the two worked up a sweat in the ring, trading banter and punches. Will was careful to pull his punches and not aim for Brad's head. As a former professional middleweight boxer, Brad had sustained far too many head hits and concussions, ending his career by his early thirties.

Brad was the oldest of our group. In his mid-forties, he worked in construction, running the firm that'd converted the warehouse into a gym for Henry's father. I could hear his crazy laugh as he taunted Will over a punch that didn't land. The older man was light on his feet and more agile than his bulky frame suggested. His grey hair gleamed with sweat under the bright lights.

"Hey, Daddy Bear," I called out to him and he turned to face me. "Go easy on Will. I need him in one piece for a client meeting on Monday."

Brad just grinned at me. "No promises, Baby Bear." I didn't love the nickname, but refused to stop calling him Daddy Bear. The name suited him too much.

Pete was spotting me as I lifted some weights. He and Henry were the same age, both in their late thirties, and the two had met in the military after being assigned to the same unit. They had such a tight bond, almost like they'd been friends for life.

After being injured and losing his lower right leg just below the knee, Henry had missed Pete and his friendship more than being in the service. It was a particularly rough time for him with the death of his mother and the breakdown of his marriage. Pete had been due to re-up but left the military and moved hundreds of miles to be near Henry instead. They'd lived together for a while until Henry met Gemma, his girlfriend of two years. The friction that she caused between Henry and Pete had Pete moving out to get some space. I'd only met her a few times and wasn't very keen on the woman. Pete outright hated her.

Henry and Pete only ever argued over Gemma and today was shaping up to be a big one. Gemma insisted we call her Gem because she hated her full name, but it didn't feel right to me. I hardly knew her, we weren't friends, and what I did know about her wasn't good. Gemma wanted more of a commitment from Henry. A ring or moving into his place; it seemed either was enough for her. Henry, though, was reluctant to take that step, and kept dragging his heels over offering her more, and Pete was all too happy to point this out. I could see Henry as he walked the gym floor checking on people and cleaning off equipment. Time and time again his gaze was drawn to Pete, who was steadfastly ignoring him.

As Pete leaned down to help rest the bar at the end of my set, his green eyes caught mine. My heart hurt for the pain that I saw in their depths. "You okay man? Wanna head out early? The others can catch up later if you want."

Like how Will was closer to Brad, I seemed to have more in common with Pete. Knowing him, it was easy to tell there was something off. I got the feeling that Pete just needed someone on his side, to really listen. Henry had complained over and over about how much Pete seemed to hate Gemma, but couldn't give us a reason why. Now it felt to me that Pete needed to get it out, to tell someone why she bothered him so much.

His face softened with something like relief. "That'd be great. Can I grab a quick shower first?" he asked.

I sniffed at my pits and laughed, "Yeah, I need one too or we're never getting served. Gimme fifteen and I'll meet you at reception." He nodded before heading off to the showers and I watched as Henry followed.

I approached the sparring ring and called, "time out," which probably wasn't the right terminology but I hated boxing, hated any sort of violence really. More so after Jason, not that he'd been the first to use his fists against me, just the most persistent. I'd been in a bad place after my breakup with Jason and been given some therapy but I knew that I'd have to let a new partner know that some things could trigger me. I probably needed to seek out more counseling, but didn't feel in the right frame of mind for it yet.

The guys paused and turned long enough for me to explain that I was heading out early with Pete. Will gave me an approving smile and quick head nod in acknowledgement, which left me with a happy buzzing feeling for having gained his approval. I frowned at myself for caring so much as I headed to the locker room.

A quick shower and change out of my sweaty gym shorts and shirt into a clean plain light blue shirt, black skinny jeans, navy hoodie and my favorite high tops, and I was ready to head out with Pete.

Henry's, "Pete, wait!" in a plaintive tone still rang in my ears as we left the gym. I was determined to be a good friend to Pete and really listen though I was pretty sure I knew what was going on. Call it intuition or whatever, but I was pretty sure I'd known since I'd met them.

We were silent until we got to the bar and grabbed our usual booth. It was still relatively early, so the place was quiet. The music was low to allow people to chat as they enjoyed bar snacks and meals with their drinks.

I loved the vibe of this place. It didn't try too hard like some places did to fit in a niche or theme. Simply decorated with a lot of heavy dark wooden furniture, it had a calm atmosphere. We sat in silence until our orders were taken and I let him get himself together. Pete was the first to speak. "You know, don't you?"

I hesitated, shrugging a little. "I guessed a while ago but recently, I dunno, it seemed more obvious. You haven't told Henry?"

He snorted, his shoulders hunched with defeat that seemed to permeate every inch of him. "Told him I'm in love with him? No. There's never been the right time to tell my best friend about how I feel. I've been in love with him for years. Him getting injured damn near killed me. Gem wants to out me, though. I think that's part of her problem with me, y'know."

It was as if the dam had burst and the story of it all came flooding out. I hurt for Pete, for the love he had for Henry, thinking that he would never be loved back. He went through the times that he thought maybe it wasn't all one-sided and that Henry was just holding back because he hadn't been with a guy before. Yet Pete made these times sound like the worst of times because he doubted they were real, that hope had manifested them in some sort of fever dream.

Then Gemma had come along and driven a wedge between them. Henry had seemed besotted with her at first and felt that she could do no wrong. Pete had been determined to like her despite the jealousy he felt. It wasn't her fault that Henry didn't want him.

Unfortunately, she disliked him immediately. The more time she spent with Henry and then with Pete as they still lived together, the worse things got for Pete. She seemed to see right through him and took more and more of Henry's time, so Pete was increasingly sidelined. After a few remarks he had decided to move out, wanting desperately for Henry to beg him not to. Even with him out of the way, she wasn't happy, always interrupting when they planned to hang out.

"If he gives her what she wants, I think that'll be the end of our friendship. We're already struggling. It isn't like us to fight like this and I hate it. Gem is fighting dirty, she keeps getting in his head about me and telling him that I give her looks, or that I made a pass at her." I scoffed at that last bit and he lifted an eyebrow at me. "Seriously! Henry laughed at that one though and told her that even though I'm bi, I lean towards men and she isn't my type. At all." He laughed. "She was so offended!" He chuckled some more and I couldn't help but picture her indignant face and laugh too.

Sure, Gem was cute, maybe a couple of years younger than my twenty nine, petite with a ton of that redhead attitude. Gorgeous chocolate brown eyes that she totally knew how to work to her advantage, and charming when she wanted to be. A politician through and through, she worked for the mayor.

There had been something about her I hadn't liked the first time I'd met her. She was already a fixture in Henry's life by then, and I was the new guy though so I kept my opinion to myself. Bit remarks back even when I heard her make a couple of homophobic comments. I didn't think she was a bad person, just sheltered and maybe a little immature. She had chased Henry pretty hard from what I'd heard. Something that Brad had found hilarious.

"What're you going to do?" I couldn't help but ask. Dealing with Pete's problems took my focus off mine and I wanted to help him. It'd been a long time since I had a circle of friends. Especially guys, as Jason had been horribly jealous of any guy speaking to me, and had slowly cut me off from any friends I had.

He shrugged. "Not sure, to be honest. I'm thinking about going traveling for a bit. Maybe some space will be good." He paused, considering. "He needs to decide for himself what he wants. If she's it, then fine. If not, then great. Thing is, he keeps involving me in it like I'm a part of their relationship. I can't choose her for him because I don't think she's good enough. She's a sweet girl when she wants to be, but he isn't in love with her. If he was, he wouldn't be asking my opinion. It isn't fair to ask me."

He sounded so frustrated and I could only give him a sympathetic glance before we were interrupted by the others coming in. Pete looked confused to see Henry with them. It was much earlier than usual for him to be joining us. Often, he had to wait until closing and clean down which was over an hour away. We'd have had a couple of beers by the time he arrived.

Henry dropped into the booth with a groan of exhaustion next to Pete. Making the other man shuffle along to avoid him sitting in his lap. He sat closer than was necessary as if penning Pete in would keep him there if he wanted to leave. His face looked pinched and tiredness sat heavy on him.

Will sat next to me, leaving a respectable distance between us, though I could smell his cologne and the scent of his shampoo from his freshly-washed hair. Brad made a face that no room had been left for him before he shuffled off to get a chair to put on the end, which was Henry's usual place.

I watched as Pete and Henry seemed to have a silent conversation before they both slumped in defeat looking away from each other. Clearly, they'd reached a stalemate.

Will gently poked me in the side to get my attention and when I glanced up, he gave me a questioning look. I shook my head, unable and unwilling to get into it. Everything that Pete said was staying with me. My friendship with him came naturally. Why couldn't it be the same with Will?

Eleven - Will

After a couple hours in the bar, a few beers and some snacks, Brad made his excuses to go home to his husband. He'd been on his phone for the last hour texting, or *sexting*, judging by the heat in his eyes. Pete had practically leapt up and decided to go with him. They lived close enough to each other that they could share an Uber.

Part of me wanted to check in with Henry. He hadn't seemed quite right all night. He was still laughing and joking around, but he didn't include Pete as much even though he was pretty much in the guy's lap. Pete looked distinctly uncomfortable and kept engaging Andy in quiet conversation. Mostly though, I wanted Andy to myself. He and Pete had gone off together, Pete obviously needing someone to talk to, but he then had taken all Andy's attention for practically the whole night. I was aware that I sounded like a spoiled brat not wanting to share a toy. Not that Andy was a toy. Inside,I was rolling my eyes at myself. I was being a dick. Our friends were going through something and needed us to support them.

It struck me as funny all of a sudden. I'd spent so long avoiding relationships, even decent friendships because of all the shit I'd been through. Until Andy anyway, then he'd come along and decided that he was going to break down all those walls. He'd given me a great group of friends. People that I was sure I could rely on. That would be there for me the way my old friends should have been when things all went to crap, instead of vanishing into the ether.

Henry may have questionable taste in women. Gemma was the definition of hard work, but he was a solid guy with a wealth of experience. Completely reliable and fair. Pete was quiet, some would say withdrawn, but I think his last year of the military without Henry had messed him up a little. He didn't have any family and Henry's parents treated him like another son. So he got what it was like for me to be cut off from half of my family. I hadn't even told Andy all that stuff yet but somehow Pete had pulled parts of it out of me. Brad had traveled the world in his boxing career and knew all sorts of things and people. Nothing shocked him and he was chill to be around. Out of the group, aside from Andy, he was the one I gravitated towards normally. It didn't matter that he was quite a bit older than me; we just got each other and he was easy to be around on days when people in general just pissed me off.

After the others had left, I noticed Henry making a face at his phone. "Everything okay?" Andy asked him.

"Yeah, just Gem. I told her I was out tonight but she wants to come over." I'm pretty sure he didn't want us to see how utterly thrilled he was failing to be at the idea of spending the night with his girlfriend. Yet instead of staying and talking it out with us, he checked his phone again and decided to go meet up with her.

Making a quick exit, he left me alone with Andy for the first time since we had dinner last week. I wasn't sure how to navigate this whole "friends" thing. Despite what he thought, our hookups had meant a lot to me. He was the first person I'd been with more than once since Ethan decided to sleep with my brother. After that, it'd been a string of one-night stands, but only after almost a whole year of just my hand.

As cold as it sounded, I didn't need another person in my life. I didn't need to be half of a couple or a third in a trio or whatever. Most of the time I was happy to be on my own. Sometimes I would get a little lonely, so I'd call my mom or my sister and we'd hang out. Until Parker's, I didn't get a whole lot of free time while working six day weeks and ten or even twelve hour days. Having drifted from or blocked most of my old friends, there weren't many people for me to call on the little time off that I did have.

Instead of hanging out with people who were liable to stab me in the back while being nice to my face, I'd learned to be okay on my own. My mom had been delighted when she found me drawing and sketching again. We had a cabin outside of the city that sat on the shore of a lake and she encouraged me to go up there as often as I could. She made sure that Alex and Charlie knew it was off limits.

Being unable to go to the beach house was the cost of having the lake to myself. Suited me fine really, sand got places it had no business being. Before everything with Andy, I'd started going up to the lake again and on any weekend where we weren't together, I would escape the city to hike and sketch.

"Hey." I caught Andy's attention from the TV screen he'd been watching as he turned to look at me. "My family has a cabin outside of town, a couple of hours away. D'you think you and the guys would want to take a trip up? Spend maybe Friday and Saturday, then come back Sunday? The weather's getting cooler, but it's still fine to hike and I think there's stuff to do in the surrounding area. Brad could even bring his husband if he takes the master suite. Either Henry and Pete or you and me would have to double up though, unless someone doesn't mind sleeping in the den."

"Seriously? You have a cabin we can go to?" Disbelief was all over his face and in his tone. "Oh! We should make a long weekend of it. Take a half day Friday and have Monday off, or work remotely." He looked absolutely thrilled at the idea and it warmed me that I could make him so happy with such a small thing. Maybe this being friends thing could work.

Twelve - Andy

I'd half thought that the Friday night hangouts were all I was going to get from Will outside of work and the gym. Thankfully, I was mistaken. He'd called me late Saturday morning explaining that the Field Museum had a new exhibit he wanted to see, and asked if I wanted to go with him. I reminded myself often as I showered that this wasn't a date. Friends went places together. The exhibit sounded great, so I suggested we get lunch first then walk it off round the gallery.

The day was cool but dry, so I threw on my favorite red hoodie over a dark blue long-sleeved t-shirt. I found a pair of black cargo pants to put on instead of my skinny jeans. I wanted to be comfortable while we were walking around. My red Converse were found under my bed. I didn't want to look like I'd tried too hard, but I wanted to look good at the same time.

Nerves filled me. Despite all the time we'd spent together, we'd never done anything like this before. I didn't know all that much about Will, only catching glimpses of who he really was underneath the personas he adopted. That Will was someone really special, I could tell. It wasn't just wishful thinking; I was sure there was a side to him that I could really care about, maybe even love. And I hadn't thought about risking loving anyone for a long time.

Since we couldn't have the relationship that I really wanted with him, I was going to be the best friend that he ever had. Which sounded slightly crazy when I thought about it. Friendship with Will didn't seem like a bad substitute for what we had before. I just had to forget about how he tasted, how his cock felt inside of me. The feel of his skin on mine and the sounds of his moans in my ear. To swap physical intimacy for hopefully something better.

***

I returned home hours later, exhausted but hopeful. At lunch, there had been a lot of lulls in the conversation like we weren't sure what to talk about and it'd left me worried. When we got to the museum and Will paid for our entry, my heart had started to beat double time. It felt like a date and we both seemed to make an effort to steer it away from that territory by talking about stuff from work. That seemed to break the ice and after that it was easy.

We spent hours looking at the exhibits, particularly the Greek items they had on loan from Crete. Will told me that he'd been to the places where the urns and jewelry had been found. His father had taken the whole family on vacation to see where the extended family still lived. He'd met great aunts and uncles that he hadn't known existed.

It was strange to hear Will talk about his family. I knew he had brothers, but he didn't talk about them at all. His relationship with his dad had clearly been complicated. If he spoke about his father, it wasn't with the same affection as when I spoke about my mom. When he spoke about his childhood, there was a mixture of warmth and frustration there that I didn't understand.

Exhausted, I flopped down on the sofa before leaning to fish my phone out of my pants pocket to order dinner. As hungry as I was, there was no way I was cooking. I was too tired for that. Unlocking my phone, I noticed a text from Will.

Will: Had a great day. Thanks for coming with me.

Smiling at the message, I scrolled through the options before placing an order for delivery. Not wanting to look too eager, I waited a minute and then replied.

Andy: Thx for inviting me.

Andy: My pick next time?

I fully expected to wait for a reply, but one came back almost immediately.

Will: I thought I'd pick tomorrow and you can pick next weekend *wink emoji*

So that's how it is then? I couldn't help but laugh before texting back.

Andy: Sure, sounds good

Dropping my phone, I smiled to myself. It was only a couple of minutes later that my phone started to ring from where I'd left it on the sofa. I half expected it to be Will making plans for the next day. It was almost a disappointment when it was Abby instead.

"Hey you," she said cheerfully when I answered. "How've you been?" We chatted for a while just catching up on things, and I tipped the delivery guy extra because I was still listening to Abby tell me about the director she had run afoul of at work. I didn't want to look rude to the guy. Abby was still ranting about the director, though. Apparently their artistic vision didn't match the initial drawings my sister had drawn up. Then there were issues getting the right fabric since the stuff they had was see-through in a bad way under the bright stage lights.

I loved how Abby told stories. Picturing the way her hands moved as she talked and all the expressions on her face made me miss her. It'd only been a little while really, but I needed to make time for her, too.

"So," Winding down, she quickly changed the subject, "what's happening with you? I haven't heard much from you lately."

Dammit, I didn't really want to go into the whole friends with Will thing. I was sure that she'd think it was a terrible idea and really, really deep down, I knew that too. "Just living the quiet life, Abs. Work and the gym. Not much else, to be honest." Straight away, I knew that wasn't going to cut it. Twin sense would tell her I was evading or some crap. I'd never been able to hide a thing from her.

"Uh huh." *Shit.* "Spill the tea, Andrew Barker." *Fuck,* I was being full-named.

So I spilled the tea.

As expected, she thought it was a terrible idea and that I was going to get hurt when Will couldn't, or wouldn't, give me what I wanted. We hung up before it could end in an argument. To be fair, I got her point but it still pissed me off. I knew what I was getting into, what I was risking. At that moment I totally got Pete and I felt so bad for him. He didn't have all the memories like I did, of all the times I'd been with Will. Of how well we fit like we were made for each other. He did have something better though, a solid friendship.

Thirteen - Andy

Sunday was a beautiful early fall day. The high temperatures of summer were giving way to the easy warmth that occasionally stuck around for most of October. I met Will for brunch, a term that he hated, I thought with a smile. I'd endured a whole lecture about brunch and putting together two meals like that from a very grumpy Will. It shouldn't have been adorable, but it was.

It looked like he'd just crawled out of bed. There was a distinctly rumpled air to his appearance. He was useless without two coffees in him, he admitted, and sure enough once that second coffee hit his system, he chilled out dramatically. I left a bigger tip for the young waitress, sure that she'd caught at least some of his rant.

Will confessed that what he'd planned for us to do wasn't an option, so we had to come up with another plan. We batted about ideas for today that had included a run after we had digested our food a little. I gave a shudder at the idea of running willingly. Yes, I went to the gym, but I preferred the bike or swimming for cardio, thanks. I only ran if I was being chased, but since it was his weekend to choose, I would've gone on a run, but I wouldn't have been happy about it though. He took pity on me, presumably seeing my initial reaction, and took that off the table as a suggestion.

I honestly didn't care what we did as long as I got to spend time with him, so we settled on walking through the massive outdoor market that had sprung up a couple of blocks away from Will's apartment. I'd spotted an arcade further down the street and suggested we go in after. When I was younger, I loved going to the arcade with my friends.

"I've never been to an arcade," Will said, pulling me out of my thoughts.

When what he said registered, I stopped in my tracks and gaped at him. "What? Why not?"

He shrugged. "Just wasn't a thing we did. At home we had a games room, so my friends came to hang out at our house."

I stopped his progress towards the market, pulling on his arm. "Let's go now, then. The market can wait. We might be hungry for snacks by then."

He rolled his eyes at my mention of food. "You can't be thinking of eating again so soon."

I laughed, but it wouldn't be long before I was hungry again, though I'd probably skip dinner to make up for it. That or go for a swim to work it off. Instead of telling him that, I gestured to all of me. "It takes a lot to keep me looking this good!" I finished with a wink and laughter burst from him.

"Fair enough."

After hours in the arcade thoroughly beating Will at every game, much to his amusement, we walked to the market. My stomach growled and Will rolled his eyes. "Snacks first, then let's explore?" I nodded my assent.

The market was crowded, claustrophobic, stifling and so awfully loud I couldn't talk to Will. He leaned in. "Let's grab food and head to the park. I need to get out of here."

"Good plan!"

Will seemed to be struggling nearly as badly as I was. Panic was trying to settle in, but strangely, seeing Will suffering right along with me made it easier for me. Like I had to be strong for the both of us. I looked around briefly, but saw lines at all of the food stalls inside before I remembered the taco truck that liked to set up at the entrance to the park.

Taking Will's hand, trying not to react to how good it felt to be touching him again, I pulled him to the exit, and he followed me without question. Outside, I pointed to the park and the roof of the taco truck that I could just about see and I dragged him along behind me.

Letting go of his hand was difficult as we drew up to the truck. It felt so natural for us to be touching like that. A casual sort of intimacy that I'd often longed for in other relationships. Jason didn't like to hold my hand. He preferred to have his arm around me, a proprietary hand often running along the skin of my hip and lower back to the top of my ass.

Mark, an older guy that I'd dated near the end of college, had been the complete opposite. He wasn't out, and expected me to respect that by walking a pace behind him so that it looked to the casual observer that we were just two people who happened to be going to the same place. I later found out that this was because he was married. To a woman. They also had children. When he attempted to explain, he denied being gay, or even bi. Mark thought I'd be like the others he'd been with before and not mind being a bit on the side, a kept boy, but I didn't want a sugar daddy and ended it. I didn't date for a while after that. Mark had said some uncomplimentary things about me which had left me crushed.

After wolfing down some of the best tacos I'd ever had, we walked a circle around the park just talking about anything that came into our heads. I teased him relentlessly about preferring DC to Marvel, unsure on how that subject even came about. He mocked me for my new love of BTS. I was blaming Abby for that one, but I thought some of them were pretty hot. I hadn't even heard of the band that he really liked, The Maine. He played me some stuff from his phone though, and I loved the singer's voice and promised to listen to them properly at home.

We stopped to sit on a bench overlooking the small pond, people-watching and making up stories about what they were doing. Will cracked me up with his versions of what he thought people were doing. Some were a little dark, others utterly ridiculous.

Will asked a lot of questions about my life, family and how I grew up. I didn't mind talking about my mom, though thinking of her sometimes did make me want to break down. The pain of her loss was still as sharp as it had been when it was fresh a decade ago. It stunned me to think that November would bring the ten year anniversary of her death.The woman had been my hero growing up. She held together our small family with sheer determination at times, working multiple jobs after our dad had walked away.

To keep the mood from dropping too far, I told him about things that me and Abs would get up to when left to our own devices. He cracked up at makeovers gone wrong, cooking disasters and "Stabby", my sister's mean persona that came out when she was feeling particularly evil. Quite honestly, the woman still scared me. I assured him he did not want to be on the receiving end of a Stabby rant and rave.

In return, I was told stories of his sweet little sister Matilda, or sweet until she hit puberty and became vicious, so he said. It seemed that he relished that though, as his eyes lit up when he told me some of the ways she had gotten back at people that'd hurt her. She was quite a bit younger than him, but they seemed to be close. I was glad that he had someone because often, to me, he appeared lonely. Like something was missing.

We spent some time making plans for heading up to the lake house that Will's family owned. It was a little intimidating being around someone who was so rich, especially after talking about my humble beginnings. And it wasn't exactly like I was rolling in it now.

Mom's death had been sudden, a car accident on her way home from work and a drunk driver. She'd had decent life insurance so we paid off and then sold the house. We both had partial scholarships and loans to pay for college. We paid off the loans and used the remainder of the house sale money to pay for the rest of college.

A degree in design was more expensive than mine. Abby needed equipment and things like fabric, so I gave her a bigger share of the money and took out a loan for her final year. She'd wanted to drop out, knowing she couldn't afford to finish without the loan, but couldn't get one. A bank wouldn't loan her a thing, unsure of when she would be able to pay it back. I'd had employment interest and internships though, so a loan was no issue for me. It'd been nothing to me to make that investment in my sister's career. Abby was the only family I had left, so she was worth every cent.

I wondered if the disparity in how we were raised would change how he saw me. Will was clearly privileged. He'd been to a private school before being kicked out due to anger issues. It surprised me to learn that he'd been to anger management therapy. He seemed so outwardly calm and in control, so whatever he had learned there had obviously helped.

The guys were all in for the weekend after next, with all of us opting to stay for the Monday, too. I did wonder how work would take it with having both project managers away at the same time, though with my team, there would be no issues as Clara often stepped up when I was away for whatever reason.

"Is this going to change things at work?" I asked him.

"What do you mean?"

"Well, everyone in the office jokes about us, you know that right?" He nodded, "So, they've noticed us being friendlier at work." They already had. Clara had been trying to get the details out of me all week. "And now we're going away at the same time...." I hoped he would get what I was trying to say. They would think we were dating especially with how differently we had been acting.

"You think they're going to assume we're dating?"

"Well yeah, are you okay with that? If we say we aren't, they won't believe us."

He shrugged. "Doesn't bother me. We know where we stand. We don't have to lie like we would've before, if they'd figured it out. We can honestly say that we're just friends, nothing more."

Fourteen - Will

Having Andy as a friend was great, but frustrating as hell. I missed sex, particularly sex with him. My new friend was prone to touching me all the damn time which, yes, I loved, but it didn't help things at all. I remembered vividly the feeling of him holding my hand the other week, how our fingers had laced together so he couldn't lose me in the crowd. I'd never met anyone who could read me as easily as he seemed to, knowing exactly what I needed before I knew myself.

Waking up hard this morning highlighted an issue for this weekend. We had to share a room at the cabin. On hearing about our "boys" trip, Gemma had insisted that she come along or Henry wouldn't be able to go. She'd made such a big fuss that I felt embarrassed for both her and Henry. I'd ended up extending her an invitation so that we wouldn't have to miss out on time with him. This unfortunately meant that Pete would have to sleep in the den and I would have to share. With Andy. The guy that still featured in all my sexual fantasies of late. Andy sharing with Pete was out of the question, the caveman side of me wouldn't allow it, or I would've slept in the den instead. I didn't want to share with Pete, either. We got on fine, but I guess I just wanted to keep Andy close.

Deciding that I needed to get some relief before packing up, I reached into the drawer of my night stand for the prostate massager that always worked to get me off quickly. I was mostly a top but I was happy to bottom on occasion. It'd been a while, though. I'd thought about asking Andy if he would top me a couple of times, a sure sign that I trusted him. Our encounters didn't allow for that though, they were often hasty frotting sessions in the showers at the gym, sneaky blow jobs pretty much everywhere, or quick fucks that didn't waste a lot of time on foreplay. There were times that I really wanted to be able to take my time with him, explore every inch of his body. Then I wanted to hand over control and let him take me apart.

Grabbing up the lube, I covered a couple of fingers with it before running a lubed finger around my hole. Pushing in slowly, there was still a faint burn from the penetration. One finger became two, and then I switched my fingers out for the well lubricated toy. Pushing it in and out a couple of times first to get used to how it stretched me, then just for the sensation of being filled. I switched it on low before lubing up my other hand and stroking my dick. My thoughts turned to Andy, the feel of his skin, the tight heat of his hole around my cock. Before long, I came, spilling over my fist, to the memory of the first time we had sex.

A few weeks after our first kiss, I still felt the sting of rejection. I'd spent more than a little time thinking about it and had thought of a way for us to both get what we wanted. He didn't want just a one night stand and I didn't want a relationship, but there was a compromise. If we could keep it casual, we could finally give in to the heat between us. Just getting him to agree would be the problem.

We were still meeting at the gym and it'd been a tad uncomfortable the first few times since the kiss. Outside of work it was pretty much the only place I could get Andy alone without appearing at his place.

He was just about to head out when I pulled him aside. "Can we talk?"

He looked wary. "Sure."

Not wanting an audience, I suggested we go on ahead to the bar and talk on the way. Straight away, no preamble, I suggested a casual arrangement. I'd stunned him into silence and he stood staring at me. After a minute he said, "Let me think about it, okay?"

While I was disappointed he didn't want to leap at the arrangement, I got that it was a big deal. We had to think of work and our friends, too. It'd be weird, disastrous even, if it ended badly.

After a few drinks at the bar with the others, I decided to head home. Except as soon as I went outside to grab a cab, I got a text from Andy with his address and the instruction to wait an hour before coming over.

Instead of going home, I waited in a different bar down the street from the one the others were in, nursing a whisky and trying to settle my nerves. Eager, and not leaving him space to reconsider, I turned up at his apartment early. A move he clearly had expected as he buzzed me up and was standing at the door, waiting for me, barefoot in comfortable looking sweats and a thin t-shirt.

I only waited for a yes to my "are you sure?" before I crashed my lips against his, moaning at the taste of him, mint with a hint of the beer he'd drank earlier. I pushed my tongue into his mouth to get more of that addictive taste. My hands ran over him, pulling at fabric as he walked backwards to the bed. His hands roamed my body, equally eager to rid me of my clothes as I was of his. Coming up for air, I gave him a smirk before pushing him back onto the bed and climbing on top of him.

Resting between his open thighs, I skimmed his torso with my fingertips, heading for the waistband of his sweats. Pulling them off over his hips, I couldn't help the moan that escaped as I noticed he was bare underneath as his length slapped against his stomach. Not quite as long as me, his rigid dick was thick and the thought of him inside me had me letting out a gasp. Hearing the sound, and seeing my reaction to him naked beneath me, his eyes darkened and his tip leaked precum.

Sitting up, he reached for the button of my jeans, slipping his fingers into the gap to stroke my achingly hard cock as he carefully drew down the zip. Running his hand over my bulge again, he ordered, "off!" before resting back on the pillows to watch me undress. Standing, I nearly fell on my face in my haste to comply and chucked the last of my clothes behind me without a thought as he snickered at me.

Crawling up the bed to lean over him again, I took his mouth in another deep kiss, one hand grasping the back of his neck as I dominated him. Swallowing his gasps and moans, I rutted against him, his hips coming up to meet mine. I needed to be touching him everywhere, only the tingle of my orgasm making me slow down.

Maneuvering us until I was resting against the headboard with Andy in my lap, I took our cocks in one hand, stroking us together as the other brushed along his crease. My lips roamed his neck as I asked, "What do you want?"

"You, in me," he whispered before ducking down to explore my nipples with his tongue. I gasped at the sensation as he bit one, and then the other, feeling the echo in my balls. I let out a small breathless laugh. "I'm not going to last if you keep doing that."

"Condom is on the nightstand, I stretched myself while I waited." He said that last part with a cheeky grin and I could only moan at the mental image of him fingering himself open, knowing that he was doing it for me.

Quickly grabbing up the condom and putting it on, I added more lube as he got on all fours. Lining my cock up at his hole, I gave him a last chance to back out. "Fuck me now or get out!" he demanded, and the pushy side of him was a real turn-on. Not knowing how much prep he had done, I took my time pushing in. I nearly came as soon as I was fully seated, hips against his ass. The grip on my dick had my eyes rolling back in my head. Pausing and desperately trying to push back my impending release, I stroked my hands down his back and along his sides to his gorgeous full ass, grabbing a handful.

"Move! Please...I need you to move," he grunted. My thrusts started out careful and slow, but before long Andy was crying out for me to go "harder," and "faster." Sounds of grunts and moans filled the room. The smell of sex and sweat. The feel of skin slapping against skin as I pushed harder into him. I pulled him up against me, one arm around his chest, hand against his throat, holding him in place as I thrust up into him, grunting against his neck between kisses and bites. Feeling close to the edge, my other hand wrapped around his cock and used his precum to ease each stroke.

He gasped, "There!" As each drive of my cock inside him hit his prostate and I focused on that spot, wanting him to love this as much as I was. This was perfection, I wanted to stay here forever, surrounded by him. Thrust after thrust, until it sent him over the edge. His sounds of pleasure coupled with the way his muscles clamped down on me quickly had me following him, spilling into the condom. It seemed endless, wave after wave of bliss. After a few more jerking thrusts, I stilled, leaning against him and trying to remember how to breathe. I couldn't think, couldn't talk, unable to remember an orgasm that intense.

Trying to be gentle as I pulled out, I helped Andy lay down and smacked a quick kiss on his lips. "Bathroom?" He pointed in the direction of a door I hadn't noticed. In the small room I quickly disposed of the condom before searching for something to clean up with. Wiping myself off a bit with a cloth, rinsing it and returning to Andy. Giving him the cloth, I felt awkward as I watched him clean up the evidence of our mutual pleasure. Taking the cloth from him, I returned it to the bathroom, dropping it into the hamper.

When I came back, Andy was sitting up against the headboard, wrapped in the deep blue covers. There was something wary about his expression and I felt the odd urge to soothe him. Sitting next to him, I wrapped one arm around him, the other lightly gripping his chin as I pulled him to me for a gentle kiss. Just a brush of lips against lips until it became more, his tongue meeting mine. Not ready for round two, and not wanting to give him the wrong impression of what this was, I pulled back.

"Okay?" I asked, the question meaning more than one thing. It was, "Are you okay? Was that good for you, too? Will we do this again? Will you be okay if I leave now?"

He seemed to get what I was asking. "Yeah, all good." So I dressed in between kisses and touches, finding it difficult to leave. Andy walked me to the door dressed only in his underwear making me *wish I wasn't such a chickenshit, and kissed me goodbye.*

***

Pete riding with us for the two hour drive to the cabin was both a blessing and a curse. The memory of how I'd gotten myself off this morning made it difficult to look Andy in the eye without blushing. Conversation was stilted at first with me being distracted at how close Andy was to me, with him sitting in the passenger seat of my SUV.

"Thanks for bringing me, Will. I really didn't want to ride up with Hen and Gem. They've been arguing all week about this trip. Henry is really embarrassed that she made such a big deal that you ended up inviting her."

"I'm just glad he's going to be there, it wouldn't be the same without him," said Andy and I had to agree. "We can all deal with Gem for one weekend and I'm sure she's found coupley things for them to go off and do," he commented, ever the peacekeeper. "And there's a few things for us to check out, I was looking up the local area yesterday online and made a list of stuff." The idea of a list made me smile, but Andy wasn't looking at me, having turned to try and placate Pete in the back seat.

Pete wasn't mollified. "Yeah, I know, but it's not the same. This is our first trip as a group. It would have been better without Gem." Andy reached over and squeezed Pete's knee and the familiarity of the gesture made something akin to jealousy burn in my stomach. I knew I didn't have the right to that feeling, though. Rationally, I also knew that Andy wasn't remotely interested in Pete. They had a brotherly bond; it was more that I was envious of

102

the attention and affection Pete was getting. Clearly I'd regressed to being a child again.

Needing to change the subject, I asked, "Have you met Dylan?" to Andy, knowing that Pete and Dylan got on well. Brad and Dylan liked their own space, so rather than come to the gym with his husband, Dylan went cycling with his own friends. Pete had been on a few of those trips but didn't take it as seriously as Dylan, who took part in big events.

"Just the once." Andy turned to face me. "He seems really cool, I think you'll like him. Even Gemma likes him." He and Pete laughed then. The atmosphere in the car settled again and the rest of the journey passed quickly with easy conversation.

***

The lake house was styled to look like a cabin, with wooden siding and a wood stove in the living room, but it was a two-story, three bedroomed, holiday home with few of the rustic features you would expect with a cabin. I'd never brought any friends up here before. Helena had never been here, preferring the beach house, so I was wary of their judgment as we pulled up.

Unlike my brothers and sister, I was aware of my inborn privilege. My family was wealthy and I'd been sent to the best private schools, until I was asked not to return. Under the advice of my therapist, I'd been sent to a regular school where I made real friends for the first time in my life. Hiding my family's wealth became second nature, just so that I could fit in somewhere for once for me, and not the money that surrounded me. I made excuses so my friends didn't come to my house and none of them questioned it. It was freeing to be out from the obligations of my family's name.

Andy gasped as we drew up and parked off to the side of the front door, his eyes going wide as he took it in. We were the first group to arrive, the others traveling together. Pete whistled as he took it in from the back seat. "Nice place."

We gathered up our things and some of the groceries that we had picked up. I'd put in an order to be delivered, but knew Andy would be hungry after the drive. He'd refused to eat in my car, which had made me laugh since I didn't care about crumbs. I left them to explore a bit while I packed things away in the kitchen and checked if we needed to cut wood for the burner.

We used a service to come by and check on the house if we knew we were going to be coming up, but I only asked them to make sure there was fresh bedding, instead of the usual fuel fill up and groceries, not knowing the personal preferences of the others. Andy had helped me draw up a grocery list by getting lists of allergies, likes and dislikes of the others, so we could make up a menu for the meals we planned to eat here. I'd spent hours on a video call with him the night before, mostly joking around, but also trying to accommodate everyone. I'd learned he was very particular about his coffee, which was something else we had in common.

While we had two holiday homes, Mom liked this house better than the beach. If it wasn't for Matilda needing to be in the city for school, I think she'd live out here full time. As an artist, she said that this place soothed her soul. Perhaps that's why I kept coming back here.

"Will?" came Andy's voice from the second floor.

"Yeah?" I called back.

"You might want to come up here." was the reply. Confused, I put the last of the snacks away before heading up to find him.

He was standing in the hallway between two of the rooms. "There's a little problem," he stated cautiously as I reached the top of the stairs. "There's only one bed in each of the rooms."

"What?" I just about managed to get out, heading over to the last bedroom that had its own ensuite. "No, the room I always shared with Charlie had two twin beds." He moved to stand next to me and our shoulders brushed as he peeked around the corner.

"Well it only has one now, same as all the others."

Glancing around him, I saw a very different room to the last time I'd been here. The walls had been repainted in neutral tones, the floors gleamed, the hardwood sanded back and varnished.

Pete came out of the first of the two other bedrooms to join us, pointing behind him. "Those have king beds but this one has a queen, by the looks of it."

"They added a shower room so the floor plan is different, a king wouldn't fit in here," I explained. "Before they added it, Charlie and I had to share the one bathroom with our brother. Alex got a room to himself since he's the oldest. When Matty came along, Alex was in college so didn't come to the cabin enough to need a room, he just slept in the den."

"So how do we sort the rooms?" Andy asked the question that I'd been dwelling on. Just sharing a room with Andy had been tying me up in knots, even when I knew I could've had him share with Pete. Sharing a bed was going to be much worse. There was no way in hell that he was sleeping in the same bed as Pete. I didn't want to share with Pete either and let Andy sleep alone.

"From experience, you don't want to stick Henry in the queen bed. If he has a nightmare, he could lash out at Gem. With being in a different place, that could trigger one. He needs the space to stretch out properly after he takes his leg off, too." Pete mused, he stopped to consider things, "Look, I could always share the queen with Andy if you aren't comfortable sharing."

"No," "no," Andy and I both rushed to interject and Pete smiled.

"Okay, what about Will and I sharing, and Andy in the den?" I looked at Andy who seemed to consider it before he shook his head.

"So you two are sharing. There's no chance of Brad and Dylan fitting in that bed comfortably, so the queen it is for you guys and they can have the master. Gem isn't getting that master bath." He looked between us, amused. "Cool, so where's the den?"

Sounds from outside drew our attention, signaling that the others had finally arrived. In the silence of the house we heard the slamming of car doors and the high pitched whine of Gem as she complained about the traffic.

Heading down to greet them, we heard Henry's reply. "We'd have left long before if we hadn't been waiting on you, love," he said gently. I cringed because laying blame on her wasn't the best start to their trip. Sure enough she puffed up, preparing to fight before Andy stepped in.

Holding his arm for her to take like an old fashioned gentleman, he said, "This way, madam and I will show you to your accommodations for this weekend," his tone affected as he attempted to put on airs and graces. He finished with a wink and Gemma's face softened into a smile, folding her arm with his as she allowed herself to be led away.

"Hen," Pete admonished. "Let's get through this weekend without you two bickering like kids, yeah?"

"Whatever, I didn't even want her here," Henry groused. Seemed he was joining me in regressing. Pete's slap to the back of Henry's head with a "grow up!" showed Pete agreed with me.

After unpacking and some needling from Gem about the master suite, we took the grocery delivery in and started dinner. Henry looked embarrassed as he came to apologize for not saying sooner but he and Gem were going out to dinner, already having asked to borrow Brad's car.

To be honest, it was a relief to have them out of the house. Everyone seemed to be on edge with her there, more so with how Henry was acting around her. I almost regretted having them at the cabin, even if Henry would have missed out on the trip. Henry's resentment was difficult to deal with. Pete wasn't helping, either. Every time Henry said something about Gemma, Pete would say something cutting and they'd end up bickering. This was supposed to be a chance for us all to hang out and get to know each other better. I'd thought that spending time with Andy would be great, and easier, if we were in a group. Less pressure that way.

Instead, Andy and I seemed to be taking over the roles of parents to three young kids. At least Brad and Dylan weren't causing any issues.

We grilled steaks outside and ate them at the table on the deck. There was a chiminea that we had lit and a patio heater, so even with the dark and cool late October night around us, we were comfortable outside. With the drama-causing couple out of the way for the evening, the atmosphere was relaxed and cozy. We didn't talk about anything big, just enjoyed the company.

After eating, we stayed outside but moved to the comfortable sofas. I took a seat on one of the larger sofas and Andy sat next to me with Pete on his other side. I'm not sure if he noticed it or not, but he sat much closer to me than Pete, and it warmed something deep inside me.

After a while, I noticed he was shivering slightly, so I started to rifle through the storage bin beside me to find one of the fluffy blankets that mom left there. Drawing out a deep blue fleece lined blanket, I laid it over him and Pete. "Thank you," he said with a sigh as he started to warm up. Instead of moving closer to Pete and sharing the blanket and the warmth that it gave, he drew closer to me, prompting me to wrap an arm around him and draw him into resting his head on my shoulder. Pete, on his other side, moved closer but their positions weren't nearly as intimate, which soothed the stupid jealous side of me. Andy let out another tiny sigh, probably not audible to anyone but me and those butterflies in my stomach started to riot.

I was coming to realize that friendship with Andy was going to be horribly complicated, and if he could just let me get my shit together, maybe friendship wasn't all that we would have. I wanted this. Tranquil nights in the moonlight, friends, and the quiet cabin. The peace that came from having him there, just holding him gently. It smoothed over a crack in my heart, proving that it wasn't as broken as I'd thought.

Fifteen - Andy

As we got ready for bed, nerves swarmed in my gut and my fingers trembled, making it difficult to untie my shoes and undress. Glancing up, I noticed Will was trying to look anywhere else but at me. We'd already taken turns in the small bathroom, washing up and brushing our teeth.

Don't be ridiculous, I admonished myself, *you've seen him naked so many times. He's been in you!* Rolling my eyes I finished stripping off and climbed into bed.

"This side okay?" I asked him.

"Sure,"

He put the last of his clothes on the chair near the bed before climbing in next to me. We each shuffled around a little, adjusting pillows and blankets while trying not to touch the other. As I moved position, my foot brushed his leg and he started.

I turned to face him, deciding just to confront the awkwardness. "We've seen each other naked and still managed to be friends these last few weeks. We can share a bed without a problem." I wasn't sure if I was trying to convince him or me but he turned to me, his face softening,

"You're right, we're making more of it than it needs to be." His expression turned wistful. "I haven't just slept next to someone in ages, so sorry if I kick you!" He tried to lighten it with humor, but it fell slightly short.

I laughed a little just to stop it being weird. "I've already tried to kick you, missed though." He gave a little laugh before yawning and turning over again.

"Night, Will," I turned away from him.

"Night, Andy."

It felt like I was awake half the night, hyper-aware of every breath he took, and every shift in position. I thought sleep was going to elude me entirely, but eventually exhaustion took hold. It was the only reason that I could think of for how I woke up.

Every inch of me was plastered against Will. We were on our sides, both of his arms around me, holding me firmly against him. One of them splayed against the small of my back, just above my ass, the other at the base of my neck, fingers in my hair. Our legs were entwined and his chin rested on my head as I blew puffs of air against his chest. One of my arms was around his waist, the other trapped against his chest, hand resting against his neck. It seemed impossible to be any closer to someone and I had no memory of how we ended up like this.

Attempting to pull away was futile. Will just grumbled in his sleep and pulled me closer. I tried to maneuver my arms, hoping to gently peel him off me before he woke. After being pulled closer again, I gave up and gently stroked his back, enjoying being this close to him. The warmth of him, the comfort of being surrounded by him and his smooth skin over lean muscles was intoxicating. I wanted to breathe him in forever. This is what I wanted, all the time.

I knew then that Will had been right to have a no sleepover rule, as waking up to this regularly would've fucked with my head. As it was, just having it this once, without the intimacy that sex can provide, was doing a number on me. I think Will could've asked for anything then and I would have given it to him just to stay like this for longer.

I felt the moment where awareness struck him as his body tensed. Luckily, I had stopped stroking his skin, and decided to pretend to be asleep instead to make it easier. This way we could both pretend that we hadn't gravitated towards each other in the night. As he moved away, I made myself make sleepy grumbling sounds until he got to the safety of the bathroom and my eyes pinged open. Well, shit.

***

I didn't know the etiquette, was it inappropriate to get myself off in the shower while the others were downstairs? I wasn't really sure that I cared, I'd keep quiet and the others wouldn't hear. All I could think about was how whole I felt, surrounded and safe in Will's arms. I could still smell that slightly woodsy scent that lingered on his skin from the previous day. If we were going to end each night wrapped up like that, this whole weekend would test my resolve not to be physical with him again. He was a craving that itched under my skin.

Pouring some soap into my hand, I gave my cock a firm stroke, moaning quietly. Aware that I couldn't take too long, that would be suspicious, I quickened my strokes, adding a twist at the crown. My grip tightened as my orgasm neared, already on edge from how I'd woken. I bit my lip to keep from crying out as my release hit, the evidence washing away.

Dressing and joining the others, I was relieved to see that Will was pretending that it hadn't happened. Also a little disappointed honestly, I just wanted him to want me the same way I wanted him.

The atmosphere was subdued but I was pleased to see Will chatting with Dylan and Brad. The more I got to know Dylan, the more I liked him. He and Brad were just two halves of the same whole.

Henry, Gemma, and Pete were eating quietly. Pete avoided any attempts by Henry to start a conversation by giving one word answers. Henry appeared to be giving Gemma the silent treatment and she was building up to blow, I could just see it. Trying to avoid it, I made a point to ask her plans for the day. She gave me a grateful smile before outlining the itinerary she had made.

Unfortunately, there were very few group activities on there and Henry looked about ready to pitch a fit about it. Brad drew Dylan away to get ready for the hike that we'd planned and Will looked to me for help. Pete got up silently and left the room leaving behind unbearable tension.

Surprisingly, it was Will that decided to jump in and calm the situation before I'd figured out what to say. He threw out a couple of options, trying to include Gemma in the day's plans and offering to make concessions for her, since she didn't hike. Unable to stand up to the charm of Will, she quickly agreed to the changes and practically bounced out of the room to get ready.

Will and I exchanged smiles before tucking into the breakfast he'd cooked up with Brad's help. I didn't know what to do about Henry, he seemed determined to be miserable and by extension, make everyone else unhappy.

"Henry," I started slowly. He sighed at me. "I know, I'll stop. I'm not going to ruin your weekend because mine isn't going the way I wanted." I patted his shoulder awkwardly, our friendship wasn't the same as the one I had with Pete. I didn't know if it was just because he was straight and had this view of male friendship, but he didn't welcome touches the same way as the others did. It could be a military thing, but Pete wasn't the same. I brushed the thought off. He got up to go and get ready for the day, giving my shoulder a squeeze as he walked by.

The air thickened with awareness between me and Will. I didn't think he knew I'd been faking sleeping this morning, but I was so very aware of how I just wanted to walk into the circle of his arms and stay there.

I helped clean up and pack up snacks, trying to avoid being too close to him in the small kitchen. Occasionally our fingers would brush and I could feel the tingles from the innocent touch run up my hand. We moved around each other in a coordinated dance, not needing words to ask the other to pass things.

The spell was broken by the others coming in, pulling our focus away.

Sixteen - Andy

The area we were staying at was beautiful. Picturesque, with hills and valleys that we could roam for days. As a group, we explored a few of the trails, taking lots of breaks to accommodate Gem. It was the perfect day for being outside, mild with a clear sky. Soothed by the sounds of nature, we all lapsed into silence. Only our footsteps and heavy breathing broke the tranquility.

I'd noticed before that Will didn't talk that much, seeming to prefer to observe the others than take part in conversations. I think he also needed to recharge after a while, like being around so many big personalities was taxing.

Often, I found him sketching on our breaks. He would perch somewhere and draw. Sipping water, or munching on an apple, he would trace the shapes of trees and rocks in his notebook. I was desperate to see what lay in those pages. I'd seen a few of his drawings before at work. He was gifted, utterly wasted in advertising. He should've been an artist like his mom apparently was. I noticed that he was calmer with his sketchbook in hand, a smile teasing at the corner of his lips.

We passed the day easily. The tension of the morning was gone now that Gem had been placated. When she was happy, she was a lovely woman, but I just didn't see why Henry was staying with her. They didn't make each other happy.

When we got back to the house, Gem went off to get ready for dinner. She and Henry were eating out again. Tired after a long day hiking a few of the nearby trails, I was glad we'd decided to do the same. I was relieved that we'd picked a bar with great food that came highly recommended rather than the upscale restaurant that Gem had picked.

The small town was a short car ride from where we were, so we decided to drive in and see what it had to offer. Dylan abstained from alcohol, and had offered to be our designated driver for the night which pleased the rest of us. Will happily passed him the keys to his SUV and sat in the back with me and Pete. As the smallest of the two, I ended up squished in the middle both times, and I was thankful that the journey wouldn't take long.

The beers and the shots had clearly lowered all of my inhibitions because the next morning, as I woke wrapped up in Will again, I could clearly remember the way I'd cuddled up to Will before falling asleep. Also the sleepy, tipsy kisses that we had exchanged before passing out, thankfully far too drunk to go any further.

Fuck my life! I was being the shittest friend, constantly making moves on the guy when he'd made his feelings clear. I needed to stop using Will as my personal body pillow and get a grip.

Extricating myself carefully, I gathered up my things quickly, hoping not to wake Will. Wincing slightly at the quick movements that were making my head pound, I had a brisk cool shower, minus the jerkoff session because my dick did not deserve attention this morning. He kept getting me into trouble when I let him take the lead. Dressing quickly in khaki shorts and a blue t-shirt that was just a smidge too tight, I carefully tiptoed through the bedroom and downstairs in search of a bucket full of caffeine for this headache.

"Andy!" Gem's voice speared through my head and I rubbed my temples as she approached me at the breakfast bar. "Sorry, I was wondering if you were into doing a slightly longer hike today? Maybe one of the mid-level trails? We did well yesterday with the ones that we did and Henry doesn't want to go into town again." She pouted. "What d'you think? Did you guys have anything planned? Maybe we should stay as a group?"

"Um, yeah? Maybe…I dunno if we really had firm plans. I'd made a list of stuff for us to do but it seems that a lot of the things on there are out of season now." I paused to think over what we had discussed yesterday.

Pete had hoped that Henry would want to do stuff as a group, but that depended a lot on Gem. Here she was offering, so I really couldn't say no. Me offering to adjust our plans yesterday had apparently made her thaw towards me. Not sure where I stood on that, but it was better than her being hateful, I suppose. "I think we were just going to hang out by the lake, but if you want to go on another hike then I could go for that." Her face lit up and I couldn't help but feel bad. She was trying to get on with us and desperately trying to make Henry happy.

"Will," she called, seeing him approach us in the kitchen. I tuned out of their conversation, trying to concentrate on the really important task of getting my coffee perfect, until I heard my name. "Andy thinks it'd be good. Something for us to do as a group, don't ya?"

My head raised and I met Will's eyes. I could feel a blush run over my cheeks at how I'd cuddled up to him last night. Him passing out on me was a blessing. This moment would be a hundred times more awkward if we'd fucked. The blush darkened, I could feel the heat of it and Will's smile and head tilt made it clear he knew I was thinking about the night before.

"You okay there, Andy?" he asked as he rounded the breakfast bar to stand by my side, his rumbling voice sent a shiver through me and he smirked. "You look warm." he pressed a hand to my forehead. "Nope, no fever. Something on your mind?" He winked at me and the relief was overwhelming that he wasn't going to make it a big deal. Resting a hand on my shoulder, he squeezed it as he reached over to get the coffee pot and get his fix.

Looking at Gem, who stood in the doorway watching us with fascination, he smiled and shrugged. "If Andy thinks it's a plan, I'm in. I'm sure we can get the others on board, too." Gem clapped with delight before begging me for help with packing up snacks and drinks for all of us.

Sure enough, Gem's enthusiasm was infectious, and the others were up for a longer, slightly more challenging hike. We loaded up with a decent breakfast and made sure to get the right shoes on, Gem complaining about how ugly her hiking boots were. "You'd end up with blisters in sneakers," I carefully reminded her. I didn't want to undo the bridge building that I had done this weekend.

"Fair point," she said affably. Pete quirked an eyebrow at the exchange and I gave a one-armed shrug in reply when Gem wasn't looking, not wanting to question it.

We took two cars to the starting point of the trail, not wanting to add on a couple of miles on top of the mid-level hike. Pete rode with us again, all of us just assuming we would divide in the way that we'd arrived here. "What's up with the personality transplant from Gem?" he questioned.

"No idea, but it's about time," remarked Will from the driver's seat. I was in the back trying to put a little distance between Will and I. The others had been giving us looks this morning, so I think there'd been some crossed lines the previous evening. My memory was just a little vague on details on what'd happened after the first bar, and the shots. I didn't drink a lot, often having a soda at the bar with the others, so I was a bit of a lightweight.

"I'm just glad she isn't causing drama," I chimed in. "This is our last full day here and I want to enjoy it, not listen to them fight. So if she's decided she's in a good mood, then great. Makes it peaceful, you know?" They nodded their agreements.

Since Will knew the area better than we did, our car was in the lead, with the other car following. We pulled up in the small parking lot and started to gather up our packs. Checking the route and the weather one last time, we set off.

The first little while was serene. We'd lucked out with mild weather for nearing the end of October. If it had rained at all, it must have been while we were sleeping, as there was hardly a cloud in the sky.

Brad, Dylan, and Pete were leading the group with Will and I behind them and Gem and Henry behind us. We'd walked a couple of miles, just enjoying the open air and the sounds of a river nearby, when Gem started to complain. I turned to Will to see him rolling his eyes as her words took on a decidedly whiny tone. "My feet hurt. Henry, wait up! You're going too fast for me." Henry's pace didn't seem to slow; in fact he seemed determined to pass me and Will so that he could walk with Pete, but Gem was insistent that he stay with her. She slowed, and taking pity on her, I suggested we take a short break.

"Gem?"

"Yeah?"

"You want me to look at your foot?" I knew how miserable blisters could be on an easier trail.

"Would you?" She looked like she might cry.

"Sure, let's go find a nice rock to sit on next to the river, yeah?" I took her arm and led her to a flat area that looked comfortable enough to rest on. "Will, is it your bag that has the first aid kit?"

He took the backpack off to have a look, holding it out to me. "Here you go."

"Thanks."

Gently taking off her boot and her too thin socks, I noticed that both had bad signs of chafing, but no actual blisters or bleeding. "Good news, we got them before they'd really hurt, but they've been rubbing." I looked up at her, keeping my tone gentle. She wasn't an outdoorsy person, so she didn't know any better. Considering the state of her feet, I felt my conscience twinge, I think I'd have complained sooner. "Your socks are too thin for these new boots. A couple of band aids or a bandage should help." Quickly getting her sorted out by wrapping her feet to act as a better barrier, I got her boots re-laced slightly tighter than before.

My legs were starting to cramp from the crouching. Making a move to stand, I pushed off the rock, but my left foot was wedged and I cried out as I staggered and twisted. I landed with a dull thud. Pain, sudden and sharp, flared as my head struck something, likely another rock. The world blurred for a second. I dimly heard the others shout for me, and felt hands trying to catch me.

I came back to awareness, in what could have only been seconds after I fell, as I was still on the ground. Will was kneeling on the ground by my head. "Andy? You okay?"

I winced as his fingers stroked over my head and came away covered in blood. Trying to move, I was stilled by his hand on my chest. "Don't, you're bleeding. I need to look at that and try and stop the bleeding a bit before you move."

Unable to stay lying on the damp grass, I tried to pull myself up to sit, pushing off his hand as I attempted to pull my legs up. Gasping with the pain and trying not to shout out, I gave up.

"My leg, it's stuck. Hurts," I managed to grit out through the wave of agony.

Will pulled some clothing from the backpack. He covered me with his navy jacket he'd taken off earlier, using it as a blanket, before finding a grey hoodie in the depths of the bag and making a pillow for me. "I'll get blood on it," I protested.

Will frowned. "Don't care. I'm going to try and get your foot free, okay? It might hurt. Okay, it probably will hurt, but I'll do it as quickly as I can."

White hot pain flared along my leg as Will ran his hands over my foot. Trying to wiggle it loose, I could only clench my fists and bite my lip. It was excruciating but quickly faded to a throb as Will freed my foot, placing it gently on the grass. With deft fingers, he unlaced my boot, removed my sock and examined the injury.

Quickly cleaning the scrapes and wrapping my foot and leg firmly, vomit rising with how badly it hurt, Will announced, "I think the hike is over for you. At the very least, it needs to be iced and elevated. I'd feel better if you had an x-ray." A part of me wanted to argue and not be a burden but there was no way that I was going anywhere but back to the cabin.

Will looked up at the others who had been watching carefully in silence. "I'll take Andy back to the house and try to convince him to go to the clinic in town." He smiled as he said the last part and I could only huff out a laugh. "You guys continue on if you like, Andy's fine. Pretty sure it isn't broken. Most likely a sprain and maybe a mild concussion."

"I'll help," Gem chimed in. "I feel like it's my fault and I was holding everyone back, anyway." She shrugged, like it wasn't a big deal, but I wanted to give her a hug. The poor woman looked to be on the verge of tears.

Henry approached her, giving her a quick hug and a kiss on the temple. "You sure, babe?" Giving him a short nod, she stepped back and drifted to my side.

Will pulled my attention back to him as he started to fuss over the wound on my head. "It won't stop bleeding," he grumbled.

"Head wounds bleed a lot," Pete called over. "It likely needs a couple of stitches, or to be glued."

"Right, thanks." Will muttered, pulling out dressings from the kit.

While the others all looked concerned, Will looked upset. His fingers trembled as he cleaned the cut, causing me to flinch. "Sorry," he whispered. I covered his hand with one of mine, giving it a brief squeeze.

"I'll be fine. Thanks for cleaning me up."

After doing what he could to stop the bleeding, Will packed up the remains of the kit, got his things together and helped me stand. He took my left side to take up most of my weight, his arm around my waist, mine along his shoulders. He had to stoop slightly to make it work but when I tried to move my arm, he resisted. "It's fine, let's just get you to the car, okay?"

Gemma came to my other side, putting her arm around me too, making me steadier. The others seemed reluctant to continue, but after a grumbled complaint from Will about having me standing about, they set off. Gem watched them sadly as Henry didn't spare a backwards glance.

The miles passed surprisingly quickly with Gem keeping conversation upbeat, refusing to let us sink into silence. She stripped off her coat and fleece top, stripping down to a thin t-shirt, as we reached the car, propping the coat and fleece under me in the back seat. Touched by her thoughtfulness, I pulled her to me and kissed her cheek. "Thanks, Gem."

She looked taken aback, more so, perhaps on the verge of tears as Will squeezed her shoulder as he passed. "Couldn't have gotten him down here without you."

We were silent in the car, the sounds of the radio seemed distant. On approaching the house, Will turned his gaze to Gemma next to him, "Will you be okay in the house yourself? I'm going to take Andy to the clinic." I went to interrupt him and refuse but he sent me a quelling look and I subsided. If I didn't go now, the others would insist on it later and I didn't want Will to be worrying about me all afternoon.

"Sure, no problem. Maybe I'll take a bath or something." Turning to me, "You'll let me know what's happening, won't you? So I don't worry." Poor thing looked like she was taking the blame for the whole thing on herself.

"It wasn't your fault, Gem. Just a freak accident. I'll message as soon as we get done at the clinic, okay?" She gave me a nod and a kiss on the cheek before exiting the car and heading up to the house.

***

The little town had a small clinic that fortunately, had an x-ray machine, saving us a journey back to the city. The doctor was finishing up with another patient when we arrived and I thanked whoever was listening that we didn't have to wait for her to be called out. I hated hospitals and their funky smells and sterile decor, and this clinic, while warmer, still had the antiseptic smell that brought back too many unpleasant memories. Having Will treat me with such concern was doing nothing to help me push down all the feelings I was having. He hovered over me the whole time, asking the doctor questions, making sure I was as comfortable as possible, and generally making things one hundred times worse in the process.

The doctor pronounced a sprain, assorted lacerations, a mild concussion and dealt with my freakout as she cut some of my hair to apply the glue to the wound on my head. With a laugh, she advised rest and also someone staying with me in case there were any other concerning symptoms.

After some great painkillers, we were on our way back to the cabin. Too out of it to argue, I let Will pay the bill rather than try and figure out insurance. I'd pay him back, although convincing him to let me would be an issue.

Arriving back at the same time as the others, I was fussed over a great deal, which left a warm feeling inside. Will had messaged Gem for me, and she was ready with an ice pack and somewhere to prop my leg when I was settled on the couch.

We spent a quiet evening in the house, ordering pizzas instead of cooking or going out. Henry and Gemma stayed with us but were more subdued than the rest of us, sitting as far apart as they could on the loveseat.

I felt more than a little spoiled as I sat wedged between Will and Pete on the large sofa, covered in blankets and on orders to stay put. Conversations were short lived as we all attempted to watch a movie. I couldn't pay attention, too focused on

Will's arm around me as he ran his fingers through my hair. Really not helping there, Will.

Settling into bed, there were no pretenses. We gravitated toward each other immediately, seeking reassurance. For the third and final time that weekend, I slept safe and secure, wrapped in his arms and wishing that it could be like this always.

Seventeen - Will

With Andy being injured, there weren't many things left to do at the lake house. The overcast day meant that just lounging by the lake for most of the day was out. Plus, the atmosphere between Henry, Pete and Gem was stifling. It was impossible to be in a room with them for any length of time before wanting to escape. I didn't have a clue what was going on there, though if I thought about it, I'm sure I could come up with ideas. All I knew for sure was that I wanted away from their drama, even if it meant that I had to focus on my own.

I never thought that I'd end up feeling bad for Gem, but I had to admit she had grown on me, to the point that I got a bit pissed at the way Henry was blowing hot and cold on her. Hello pot, meet kettle. I guess seeing it from the outside was eye opening.

Being wrapped around Andy, these last few nights, was the best part of the trip, and it signaled that it was time for me to sort out my commitment issues. There was no way that Andy would be content to stay friends with me if I kept acting the way I had all weekend. I didn't want to be giving off mixed signals, but there were still things I needed to confront from my past first.

The return to the city was quiet, with us all off in our own worlds. Andy was stretched out in the backseat so that he could rest his foot. I'd taken a couple of cushions from the house for him and made sure that he'd taken some painkillers with breakfast before we got going.

"Stop babying me," he'd pouted as I helped him into the SUV, settling him as comfortably as possible, aware that the journey might jostle him a bit.

"You love it," I teased, and he flushed, knowing he was caught out.

"Hey, you guys want to meet up with the others for lunch in the city when we get back?' Pete asked. he had taken the passenger seat to give Andy space to stretch out.

Andy looked at me and shrugged. "Honestly, aside from when I move, I don't hurt that bad now. I feel bad that we cut the day short for me, so I could do lunch." They both looked at me and it was my turn to shrug.

"Lunch sounds good."

***

Henry and Gem didn't appear at the restaurant for a late lunch.. Brad and Dylan were evasive when asked what'd happened on their trip back, which made me think that there'd been another fight. We hadn't talked about Gemma in the car, but I knew that both Andy and I were seeing her in a different light after the cabin. Sure, she was a little spoiled, but underneath she was quite sweet. I just hoped that Henry wouldn't string her around for much longer. His heart wasn't in it, unlike the situation with me and Andy. I just needed to get my shit together, having too much baggage to make a proper go of it with him. I wasn't unwilling, just didn't want to hurt him by ruining our second chance.

Towards the end of lunch, Pete got a text and made his excuses, looking worried. Brad and Dylan quickly followed him, clearly ready for some privacy, which left Andy and I alone. The air between us was tense, so unlike all the times we had met up recently. Some of that was the physical closeness we had shared. The kisses that we both ignored. I was just thankful that we hadn't gone further because, for now, he had to stay my friend and nothing else.

"Let's get you home so you can rest that foot." I suggested, "Do you need any help with anything before work tomorrow?" He shook his head, looking confused at my offering to help him. "I can pick you up in the morning if you aren't up for driving, just let me know."

He smiled shyly at me. "Thanks Will, you're the best."

Leaving him was difficult, so I hung about a bit. I was grateful that his apartment building had an elevator since he was on the fifth floor and those stairs would have been a nightmare with his injury. Making myself at home, I got him settled on the couch, foot up on the coffee table, and headed to the kitchen to get some ice.

Andy fell asleep not long after, his head tipped back and his mouth hanging open slightly. I watched him for a little while before deciding to help him out and get some things in for dinner and breakfast. I left a note on the table in case he woke before I returned and snatched his keys up from the bowl next to the door.

I cast a glance over the space before leaving, finding it strange that I felt more comfortable in his place than mine. He'd told me, in little stories here and there, about his sister and the work she put in, wanting to help make it a home.

He wasn't forthcoming about a lot of his past, something that I couldn't call him out on. I wasn't that much of a hypocrite. I wanted to know everything about him, even the bad parts, the things that troubled him. The visit to the doctor the day before had pulled up some red flags. When asked, Andy had admitted that he'd sustained head injuries before, but was vague on the details, shutting down on me when I'd tried to push for details. It got me wondering if anyone had hurt him, in his teen years or in relationships. Anger rose in me at the thought of anyone raising a hand to him because he was the sweetest, most gentle soul I'd ever known.

I returned just as Andy woke up, all sleep-mussed, confused, and adorable. I made us a light stir-fry for dinner and helped get him ready for bed before dragging myself away. We didn't talk much, but the earlier tension had evaporated, and I didn't want to blur any more lines than I had. My apartment wasn't far away; I could run over if he needed me.

He hugged me as I got ready to leave. "Thanks for everything, Will. This weekend…Well, the weekend was great. It's been ages since I left the city. So thanks for that, and for looking after me. You didn't have to do that."

"I wanted to, and it was great to get away with everyone. We should do it again, in the spring, maybe." I felt a little flustered at the sincerity in his voice and how he was looking at me, like I was his favorite person, ever. He deserved better. "Get some sleep," I ordered with a quick smile. "I'll be by to pick you up in the morning."

I made sure the door locked as I left to save him getting up again, and headed home. My apartment had been cleaned in my absence and I hated how empty and sterile it was. I had no emotional connection to any of the things in here, save for a few things in my bedroom. I had no stories about things I'd done here. It was just a place to sleep and keep my clothes in.

The night passed slowly as I slept fitfully, unable to drift off properly without Andy next to me. Remembering the feel of him, the citrus scent of his skin, gave me enough peace that I finally slipped into sleep.

Eighteen - Andy

The dull throbbing headache of yesterday had faded into a barely-there echo of pain when I woke. My mouth was dry and the wounds were itchy, but all things considered, I didn't feel too bad.

After hopping around and leaning on furniture to get ready for work, I was grateful that I didn't have to try and drive. My ankle wasn't up for that at all. Will texted when he reached my building and I managed to hobble to the elevator. Obviously sensing that I wouldn't make it to the front of the building under my own steam, he'd parked near the elevator doors in the parking garage and was waiting out of the car to help me.

The angel that he was had two travel mugs of coffee sitting in the SUV's cup holders and, given that the day was on the cooler side, had the seat warmers on. I moaned in delight as I got myself situated from the relief of being off my foot and the sheer pleasure of a cozy, warm car. Will chuckled at me and I smiled, happy to make him laugh. "Thanks for picking me up, I don't think I'd have managed myself."

He buckled his seat belt and made to move off. "No problem at all. What are friends for?"

It shouldn't have stung, but it did, to have the reminder. I needed it though. I knew that we'd both been blurring lines all weekend and it wasn't fair to push. Will was direct, straightforward, and I knew that if he was ready to take things further with me, then he'd say so. This had to be a not so subtle reminder to dial it back a bit.

"Well, currently, if you want to know the rankings, you sit in joint first place in the friendship league for your efforts."

I chuckled at his faux hurt face.

"Only joint first? Not first? I am very offended!" He couldn't contain his laugh. "Who's up top with me?" He asked.

"Abs, of course. Twin privilege says she's always at the top."

"Ah." he shrugged. "That I can deal with. Do I have any other competition for near the top?"

I took a second to think."Well, I'm not sure, I don't have a ton of close friends, y'know? Maybe Josh."

"That's Abby's boyfriend, right?" He cut in.

Pleased, I gave him a smile.

"Yeah that's right, He's like the brother I never wanted." I laughed. "They've been together for nine years or so."

He let out a whistle "Wow! That's a long time. Do they not want to get married?"

"Well," I started to explain, but stopped. "It's a big thing, but it's between them, y'know? So I try to keep out of it. Anyways, marriage isn't a guarantee of happily ever after. They work as they are."

He considered for a second. "You're not wrong there. Doesn't matter as long as they are happy right?"

***

I'd discovered on Tuesday night that orgasms are wonderful headache cures. A long day in the office had worn me out and I arrived home with a throbbing head. Napping didn't help and when I went to bed, I couldn't sleep. Frustrated, I'd tossed and turned as much as my sore leg allowed. The pain was fading, but movement still sent pain through me. After what felt like hours trying to sleep, I thought about checking out some porn and jerking off. It worked in the past; that floaty, post orgasm high had never failed to send me off to sleep.

Shifting through videos on the site I subscribed to (I didn't have cable, okay?), a clip caught my eye. A tall, dark-haired man, with beautiful olive skin, was pounding into a smaller blonde. Before long the guys were swapped out with me and Will, until I put my phone down altogether, wandering down memory lane.

Piecing together a scene from memories and daydreams, I created what could have happened in the lake house if we hadn't been too drunk the night we kissed to sleep. I stroked my cock to imaginary Will taking me into his mouth, swallowing me down, and letting me fuck his throat. I came picturing Will keeping my load in his mouth before sharing the taste of myself in a messy kiss. Aftershocks hit as he took it back. "Delicious," dream Will said with a smirk as he swallowed my remaining cum. I slipped into sleep, cum drying on my skin, and dreamed of being wrapped up in his arms. Of how I wished that we could do that every night.

Will picked me up and took me home on Wednesday, and our new friendship was creating a stir in the office. I loved it though; I was coming to love having Will as a friend rather than just a sex buddy. Though I wouldn't mind combining those and putting sex back on the table because my imagination was just using clips of Will and that wasn't something I could have right now. Plus those pesky feelings kept creeping up on me.

Feeling a little fragile emotionally, I got the feeling that I needed to have some space from Will. He'd been perfect these last few weeks and the time at the lake house had been idyllic. It didn't help me get over him or push him into the friend zone though; in fact, I was sure that seeing him in another light had me in danger of falling in love with him.

***

In order to put a bit of distance between us, I'd insisted that I drive myself on Thursday, plus I'd need to be able to drive to get to the support group. I think I'd gotten off lightly injuries-wise, because I was nearly back to normal. The only sign of any injury were the cuts and grazes. I'd gone to a barber to fix my hair before the support group, sick of questions of why I'd changed how I'd styled it at work. My efforts were wasted at trying to cover the slightly bald patch.

Group had been intense. One of the teens had a terminally ill parent, after already losing a sibling, and was struggling to cope. My usual coping strategies of a workout and romp with Will were both out. I'd overdone it with my ankle and came home to ice it, so no gym, and Will, well, I needed to be away from him.

Like I'd summoned him, he called me. "Hey," he said as I answered. "I'm downstairs, I brought food." Unable to turn him away since he was at my door in the pouring rain - with food! - I struggled to my feet, hobbling over to buzz him up and leave the door ajar.

"Come on up, door's open."

The smell of Chinese food preceded him. He looked relaxed and happy, if a little soggy, as he made himself at home in my kitchen, setting out containers of food and checking what I wanted.

"Why are you so wet?" Handing him a towel so he could dry off his hair, and dropping his damp hoodie over the back of the armchair, I leaned against the door frame and just watched him. Dressed in dark grey sweats and a light grey t-shirt, I don't think I'd ever seen him look so comfortable. There was no tension weighing him down.

"Walked here. Thought the rain had passed," he shrugged. "Not a big deal."

"Andy." He was standing in front of me, clearly waiting for me to move.

"Hmm?"

He gestured with a hand. "Go sit. Dinner's ready."

I blushed, embarrassed that I'd been caught daydreaming while he was trying to feed me.

"Sorry." I pulled the blanket off the back of the sofa and tried to drape it around him. He fixed a confused look on me.

136

"The heat isn't great, it comes and goes, and I don't want you to get sick." Running a hand over the soft fabric, his expression twisted to something I couldn't decipher.

Clearing his throat. "It's lovely. Abby?"

Taken aback, "Yeah, how did you know?"

"Dunno, just had a feeling."

Changing the subject because he was withdrawing a little, I asked, "Not that I'm complaining about a free dinner, but did we have plans?" I wondered if I'd just forgotten.

"Well, no. But I remembered today was support group day, and I know how you feel after them. You couldn't work out, so I thought I'd bring dinner and we could watch a movie or something. Take your mind off of it."

Something warmed in my chest at him knowing these details of my life. It was proof that he listened and understood me. "That's sweet, thank you. A movie sounds great." Pausing to think, "Action or comedy, though. Nothing sad."

He laughed. "No, nothing sad. I don't think we've reached that stage in our friendship yet where we can cry in front of each other."

I laughed and teased, "No? Damn, there goes joint first place."

He clutched at his chest. "Direct hit, I'm wounded."

By the time the movie ended, a decidedly average superhero caper, I had my feet in Will's lap and he was rubbing them absentmindedly. I'd finished eating a couple of hours ago and still felt too full to think of eating anything else. Will had stashed the leftovers in my fridge, having bought enough for four people.

"Come on you," he whispered, causing me to jerk fully awake. "Let's get you in bed." I let him move me, help me stand, and drag me over to the bed.

"Should've just stayed on the couch," I whined. "More likely to sleep there."

Will looked concerned. "You're not sleeping?"

"Well, a little, but not for long and it takes ages to get to sleep." I'm sure I was pouting a little, a hint of whine still in my voice. Sleep-deprived me was a little bit of a drama queen.

"You were sleeping fine on the couch just now," he pointed out, using logic against me.

"Only because you're here. Will you stay with me a while?" I all but begged.

He hesitated, "Andy..."

"Please?" I shouldn't have felt pleasure at how quickly he folded.

"Just until you fall asleep."

He helped me to the bathroom so I could brush my teeth, running the water to cover the noises of me getting ready for bed. The apartment was so quiet I could hear every movement he made as he put his shoes next to the door and pulled back the covers for me. The rain was still coming down outside, muting the sounds of the city and enclosing us in what felt like our own bubble. A feeling of safety and warmth filled me.

"Should I shut the blinds?" he asked.

"Nah, thanks though." Settling into bed, I turned to face him as he sat propped up against the headboard. I noticed a shiver run over him. "Are you cold?"

"Maybe a little."

"Get under the covers with me," I suggested. I wanted him closer.

"Andy….I…I don't know if that's a good idea." He looked reluctant, like he thought he should be saying no but wanted to say yes. Picking up his hand, I pulled him towards me, pushing down the covers to make room for him.

Once situated under the covers, he faced me. "Why can't I say no to you?"

I couldn't help my smile. "It's because you think I'm cute." I gave him a playful pout and batted my lashes. "That, and you feel sorry for me just now."

He huffed out a wry laugh, "Not wrong. Stop abusing your privilege." His glare was weak and ineffective and I let out a giggle snort.

"Never happening."

"I'm only staying until you're asleep, okay?"

"Okay, thanks Will."

Drifting off to sleep was easy with the sound of Will breathing steadily next to me, his face illuminated by his phone as he read the mystery book he'd been reading at the cabin. At some point, Will must have fallen asleep too, as once again, I woke wrapped up in him, startled out of sleep by a noise outside.

I took a minute to just look at him. In sleep, all of the stress he carried around all day had washed away. I longed to trace my finger along the slope of his nose. Over the high cheekbones and down to his strong jaw. Run my finger over his plush lips, the bottom just that delicious bit fuller than the top.

The noise that woke me must've done the same for him, because when I looked up at him again, his eyes were open and he was observing me with the same fascination that I was looking at him with.

My heart leapt into my throat with the look of want in those chocolate depths, the struggle twisting his expression. The moment stretched between us and I was torn between fear and need. I had a desperate need to feel his lips on mine, but could I cope if he rejected me now? Was I pushing too hard? Would this undo all of our progress?

To hell with it. After minutes of just staring, butterflies swooping in my stomach, I surged up and pressed my lips against his, sighing with relief when after a second's hesitation, he kissed me back. At first it was gentle, just lips pressing against lips. Before long, it became something deeper, passionate, as his tongue sought entry to my mouth.

Opening to him, I groaned at the taste of him, the soda from earlier underneath the usual taste of him.

I sucked on his lower lip, giving it a nip before pushing my tongue into his mouth. My hands found their way to his jaw, holding him in place as I tried to show everything I felt for him in that kiss.

His hands roamed my body before one sank into my hair and pulled my head back so that he could kiss along my jaw and down my throat. Pushing me onto my back, he settled between my legs, his hands either side of my head. "We shouldn't be doing this," he murmured against my neck.

"I don't care. I need you," I rasped, clawing at his back, pulling him flush against me, so he could feel just how much I needed this right now.

"Hmm, why can't I say no to you?" He echoed his earlier question as he let out a groan when I nipped at his throat before moving to suck a mark on his collarbone. Grinding his hips against mine, we both gasped at the sensation. Both of us were fully hard and leaking. I ached with the desire to have him over me, to have his familiar weight pressing me down into the mattress. I needed the feeling of him pushing deep inside me.

We kissed until my lips felt swollen from the abuse. I soon became frustrated with the clothes that kept me from running my hands along his skin, and tried to take them off without separating my mouth from his. Will chuckled at my growl as his t-shirt became stuck and he quickly removed both his clothes and mine, throwing them off of the bed.

He sat back on his heels just looking at me, not hiding in his expression how much he wanted me. His lust was laid bare for me to see. My cock twitched as his gaze roamed my body like a pair of hands. He shuffled back further to take his time pressing kisses from each knee up to the delicate skin where the top of my thigh met my torso. Skimming over my eager dick, kissing up my body, laving at my belly button, making me squirm and laugh, he licked over each nipple in turn, hardening each nub. My fingers tightened in his hair as he nipped each bud, making me gasp at the sensation.

I was desperate and leaking as his weight settled on me, his hard length against mine. He began to thrust, drawing gasps and moans from me. His skin was damp with sweat which eased the glide of his cock over mine. Grasping at his neck and back, I managed to get out, "In me. I need it."

He let out a guttural sound before pressing fingers to my mouth. "Get them wet."

I went to town on them, sucking and licking on his fingers like I would his cock, making him grunt. Withdrawing his fingers from my mouth, he reached under me as I tilted my hips to make access easier. One finger skimmed over my entrance before pushing in slowly.

I moaned at the stretch and the familiar burn. He didn't wait long to add another, as desperate for it as I was, his cock leaking against my leg. The other finger entered slower than the first, and the burn became sharper. Feeling my breath hitch, Will stopped, running his other hand over my skin, lightly petting me. Giving me a second to adjust before sliding them deeper again and scissoring them to open me for him.

My dick had deflated a little with the brief flash of pain, and noticing this, Will leaned down to take me in his mouth, bringing me back to full hardness. His tongue swirled around the tip of my cock, and I tried not to thrust into that perfect wet heat, or impale myself on his fingers. Doing that would have this over far too quickly. He sucked as he opened me for him, adding a third finger easily now that I was more relaxed, my cock as hard as steel in his perfect mouth.

"Will, now."

He gradually withdrew his fingers and came off my cock with a popping sound. "Lube? Do we need a condom?"

I pointed to the drawer, too far away to reach, "No condom, no one since you, still on PrEP. Unless anything has changed with you?"

He shook his head, looking satisfied that I hadn't been with anyone else. "Same, no one since you." His rumbling voice had a shiver run through me. My heart warmed that he hadn't replaced me, that there was a chance that I did mean something to him other than a quick convenient fuck.

Slicking up his hard length and pushing wet fingers into me to ease the glide, he positioned himself at my entrance. I pulled my legs up, still on my back, so that he could push in further. I gasped as I felt him fill me up, so hot and hard. He paused for a minute to allow me to adjust. The length of him hit me perfectly.

Will's cock was a thing of beauty, long, but not monstrously so. It was uncut and thick. Just the feeling of him being inside me again had my inner muscles clamping down on him, making him moan out my name. "Won't last long, if you keep doing that."

My release wasn't far off, either. "You feel too good, I'm close already."

A few careful thrusts were soon followed by sure strokes inside me. He came down over me, his stomach pressing on my cock, his arms wrapping around me as our mouths met in a messy kiss. Breathless, panting out moans and grunts, I wrapped my legs around his hips, keeping him close as he moved deep inside me.

Never had sex been like this before; this was like making love. Everything tingled with sensation. We kissed, licked and sucked every inch of skin we could reach. I couldn't get enough of this feeling. Will wrapped around me, deep inside me, whispering in my ear, "So good. Andy, missed this, I'm close."

I could only grunt as his thrusts grew harder and he pulled back a little, changing the angle, this time hitting my prostate.

"There! More!" Frantic, chasing the release that I could feel just out of reach, I began pushing my hips up to meet his.

"I'm close!" he rasped against my neck, voice wrecked. Knowing I needed more to get me there, Will snaked a hand between us to grasp my cock in a tight hold, our thrusting making me fuck his fist, my precum slicking the movement. With a twist over the tip, I let out a cry as I came hard, vision whiting out for a second. My orgasm and the way my muscles clamped down on him, had Will finding his release inside me, biting my shoulder and moaning against my sweaty skin. The feeling of his cum inside my hole had my dick twitching. A small spurt of cum joining the rest smeared between us.

Will laughed, a tortured sound as my muscles spasmed around him again.

His lips met mine again in a gentle kiss, hands cupping my head reverently, as mine stroked over his back. Time passed with us kissing and sharing gentle touches as we lay joined, coming down from the high. Absolutely satiated, I just basked in the joy of this moment.

All too soon, his softening cock slipped out of my body, the empty feeling causing me to groan. Will made to leave the bed to get something to clean us up, but I grabbed at him.

"Just grab my t-shirt." I said quietly, trying not to break the mood. Handing it to me for a perfunctory clean up, I could feel his hesitation. I dropped back against the pillows, stretching a hand out to him, "Stay," I whispered sleepily, relaxing further as he settled into bed behind me, pulling the covers over us and wrapping me up in his arms.

Just before I drifted off into sleep I muttered quietly, "Hmm, love you," already fast asleep before I registered the way Will's body tensed around me.

Nineteen - Andy

Waking up alone wasn't any real surprise, nor was the sickening feeling of hurt that I felt over it. Except it was all my fault. There was no one to blame but me. Maybe we could have awkwardly talked about things this morning, if I hadn't opened my big mouth.

I was an idiot. Had to be. Otherwise why else would I have dropped the L bomb on my "friend" just after we had just had the most mind blowing sex I'd ever had? Dumbass.

There had to be a way to fix this mess. Maybe just apologizing and having a little bit of distance would do. Ideally, I'd do it in person, but we had to go the whole day in the office together, and after the last few days of closeness, people were going to notice. So I had to sort this out before we got to work.

In between getting a much-needed shower, dressing and grabbing a quick breakfast, I must've called Will about five times. He didn't pick up; the calls going straight to voicemail. Frustrated, I couldn't think clearly and nearly called Abby for advice. She wouldn't be happy with a call this early, but she'd answer. I couldn't deal with a lecture though, so I gave up that idea.

Blowing out a breath, I decided just to text him and hope that he read it before we got to the office.

Andy: I'm really sorry about what I said last night. I know I'm pushing too hard. We shouldn't have had sex, but I don't regret it. Can you forget I opened my mouth and let us go back to being friends? Just pretend that everything after the movie didn't happen? I don't want it to be weird at work.

I perched on the arm of the sofa, my leg still stiff and sore from overdoing it the day before. Honestly not expecting a reply, it was a surprise when one came in a few minutes later.

Will: I don't regret it either, but I don't think we should do it again. Not until I can sort my shit out. I care about you too much to mess with your head. In the friendship league, you are my number one. See you at work.

Tears welled up. *His number one*? The relief was profound. Okay, so things might be a little weird, but we could get past this. Our friendship wasn't dead and buried, and he'd written *not until*, meaning we could be something more in the future. I could wait.

***

Things at the office were a little off, but not to the others. I could see it in the tense way that Will held himself, the lapses in conversations, and spending lunch alone while Will went out to eat with James instead of me. Will suggested that I order in, since I was hobbling about a bit, and he was right, but I still wished that he had stayed with me. Even if it was uncomfortable, we just needed to push through this weird patch.

Henry had texted to ask if I was up for the gym or if I just wanted to meet them at the bar. He had news to share and wanted to tell us all together. Opting for the bar, I decided to go home and do boring adult stuff, like laundry, and try not to mope about the fuck up I'd made of things. Beating myself up wasn't going to change anything.

That reply from Will had done a lot to ease the hurt of this morning, and I caught myself daydreaming about last night as I tidied up my apartment. Thinking of how at home he'd acted here soothed something in my heart. It wasn't one-sided any more.

Twenty - Will

When Andy told me that he loved me, after the most mind-blowing sex ever, I freaked out a little. Okay, a lot. To be fair, the last person that told me that they loved me, that wasn't my mom or Matty, went and cheated on me, with my brother, in our bed. The person before that, well, she married my other brother, instead of me. So those words of love had become paired with being betrayed in my eyes.

After pushing back a panic attack while Andy slept unawares, I gently pushed him off me, covered him carefully in the blankets, dressed quietly, and left.

The rain had eased slightly but I was still soaked through when I got home, having taken my time walking, just processing.

Jumping straight in the shower to warm up and then climbing into bed, I crashed hard. My spinning thoughts followed me into sleep and I dreamt of Andy, waking erect and confused before my alarm usually went off.

I needed to get out of my head, but I couldn't just head off to the gym, I had to work. Which was probably the last place that I wanted to be after yesterday. Realizing that I'd forgotten to charge my phone, I plugged it in and sat thinking about what I needed to do.

Things needed to change, I knew that. My reaction to Andy's confession would hurt him, but it caused me serious anxiety. That wasn't normal and I knew that. I needed help, preferably of the professional kind. I also needed to apologize properly to Andy. He meant more to me than he could know, and doing a vanishing act like I had would cause him pain. That was the last thing I wanted.

Picking up my laptop, I sat at my kitchen table with my second coffee and searched for therapists. I couldn't undo the past but I could make changes so that my future wasn't filled with meaningless hookups. Getting help to process what'd happened to me, the level of betrayal that I'd suffered through, could only help every aspect of my life. I'd taken a lot of anger from my childhood into my adult life, so maybe the therapist could work on that, too.

It didn't take long to find one that did an initial assessment over a video call. I sent an email asking for an appointment. Putting the laptop away, I checked my phone, grumbling when I noticed that I hadn't turned it on while it charged. Switching it on, I had a couple of missed call notifications but no messages, until a text came through from Andy.

Reading the message quickly, I took a few minutes to formulate a reply. I didn't want it to be weird, and deep down, I was so beyond happy that he loved me. It all came down to the fact that I thought he deserved better than me. I was a mess. Maybe though, I could give him a little hope that I could get over this. Show him that he meant something to me so he wouldn't give up.

Tapping out my reply, I breathed a sigh of relief. Before I put down my phone to finish getting ready for work, an email from the therapist's office came through with the offer of a lunchtime call to discuss my therapy needs. I almost laughed, but that reaction came from a father who didn't believe in discussing feelings. I'd neglected looking after my mental health for too long, but now I had someone to be healthy for.

***

Any lingering awkwardness did eventually ease over the day. Finally, I felt like I'd done right by Andy. His gentle smiles throughout the day buoyed me through my assessment with my new therapist, Dr. Arnold, who was a no nonsense woman in her fifties and specialized in relationship issues therapy. I'd blushed several shades of scarlet when she applauded me for turning to counseling for my issues. "Identifying a problem now is so healthy, William!"

Andy seemed a bit put out that I'd gone out to lunch with James, but James was meeting a date, and I was backup in case the guy didn't show. I also had my appointment and wasn't ready to share my therapy journey yet. Baby steps.

Working out without Andy around was strange and I missed him being there to ease the tension between the others. Pete and Henry I kind of got along with, but Brad seemed pissed at them both and I couldn't figure out why.

Henry wanted us all at the bar after; even Andy was coming, for some news that he had. There was no way I was going until I'd soothed some tempers. It amused me to be taking Andy's usual role, but Brad looked ready to lay Henry out.

Dressing after my shower in a black short-sleeved button up and black jeans, I took the chance to pull Brad aside.

"Everything okay, dude?" I didn't think he was going to answer, or if he did, that I was going to get the brush off, but it seemed that Brad didn't have an issue with me because he started speaking after a minute.

"Not really. I know you were busy at the cabin with Andy, especially after he was hurt, but you only saw some of how that poor girl was treated. That wasn't even the worst of it." He looked furious and I got it, I really did. Gemma had grown on me. I think a lot of the time I'd seen her through Henry and Pete's filters.

"That bad?" I winced. "I tried to include her, and she was so sweet with Andy when he was hurt. Personally, I have nothing against her. Sure, I didn't want her to come at first, but that was more because of Henry's bitching and how much Pete doesn't like her."

Brad still looked angry, but now I knew where it was coming from, and I could sympathize."It was more the attitude of Henry. Pete, I get. He's in love with Henry and crazy jealous."

That was new information. "Gem knows how Pete feels, too. She's young and is threatened by the bond those two have. Thing is, there wouldn't be a problem if she felt secure in what she's got with Henry, but he always has one foot out the door," he grumbled and I could see his point. If Gem felt that her relationship was solid then she wouldn't feel like Pete had a chance with Henry. He must be giving off some vibes that she was picking up.

"Poor Gem. Never thought I'd say that."

Brad let out a chuckle. "Never thought I'd agree. I love Henry and Pete, they've been great to me and Dylan, but this whole mess isn't fair on the girl."

"Well, I'm on the same page as you, and I'm sure Andy is too."

"How is Andy, by the way? This week's been crazy with us taking Monday off, so I haven't had a chance to check in." Brad switched gears quickly, but that's what I liked about the guy. People might've been quick to write him off as dumb, being an ex boxer, but the guy was sharp, and really cared about his friends.

"He's doing a lot better, managed to drive a bit yesterday and today, but it leaves him sore after. I think he's coming tonight, but he can't drink on the painkillers they gave him."

Brad nodded. "Good, hopefully he'll be back with us next week then."

***

"Gem and I are over," Henry announced after we were all settled with drinks in our usual booth. He looked relieved rather than cut up about it, and Pete looked sick, like the guilt of being happy about it was eating him up inside.

"What happened?" Andy took one for the team and asked the question we all wanted answering.

"You guys saw how we were at the cabin, well, when we got back, there was a fight." Brad made a harumph noise which made me think that it wasn't when they got back, more like in Brad's car. "She ended it," Henry reluctantly admitted. "She also wanted to thank you, Will and Andy, for inviting her to the cabin and making allowances for her. Just for basically being nice guys."

He laughed, which was odd in the strained atmosphere. "She also told me to tell you guys that she 'ships it,' whatever that means."

Andy let out a startling cackling laugh, "That's amazing! Is it okay if I text her? Can I get her number? She was so nice to me, I want to thank her," he asked cautiously and got a quick, "Whatever," from Henry.

I quickly sent her a text to ask if it was okay and received a thumbs up in reply, I looked over at Andy, "Gem said that you can have her number. I'll send it now."

He smiled at me, genuine happiness lighting his eyes, "Thanks Will." Sending the message over and getting a quick, "Thanks," from Andy took all of a minute. Thinking about all that Brad said earlier and how I'd gotten over my initial impression of Gemma, I decided to send a follow up text to her.

Will: Look, I'm not sorry that you and Henry are over. Yes, he's my friend, but over the weekend I didn't like how he treated you. I think you deserve better than that and hope that the next guy that comes along sees it. Thank you for making the best of a bad situation at the cabin and for helping me with Andy. Maybe once the #Andill ship sets sail, we could do coffee?

I kept an eye on my phone, watching it go on read as the others talked around me. I let out a bark of laughter at her response. I really had her all wrong.

Gem: Yas! *three laughing emojis* #Andill forever! I'm up for that.

The others were shooting me questioning glances. "Just my phone," was all I said, not wanting to go into the whole ship thing. I'd tell Andy about the hashtag thing when we were on a better footing, though. He'd love it.

Brad, deciding that he didn't care about the relationship drama any more, moved the conversation along. Between them, he and Andy were doing most of the talking, letting Henry and Pete stew about whatever was bothering them.

A commotion at the bar drew my attention and I recognized a familiar face. I couldn't be sure until I got a closer look, but I thought he might be a guy my younger brother Charlie was friends with.

"Be back in a sec," I said to the group as I got up to go and check on him. As I drew near, I saw that it was Max, my brother Charlie's best friend. It seemed like a guy standing far too close to him, holding on to his arm, wasn't taking no as an answer. To make matters worse, Max seemed a little out of it.

Walking over to him, I wrapped an arm around his waist, removing the guy's arm, and glared at the jerk. I didn't use my height to intimidate often, but it was useful here. Max was a fair bit shorter than me, with white blond hair and delicate features. Basically bait for creeps like this guy because he was so cute. Thankfully the other man got the hint, melting into the crowd.

Turning Max to face me, I put my hands on his shoulders, but had to move in closer so he could hear me over the noise of the bar. "You okay?" He sniffled a bit and I brushed his tears away with my fingers, as he shrugged. "Want me to take you home?" Max nodded.

"Will, I lost Charlie. Have you seen him? I think he left me. I don't feel well." He was slurring slightly and didn't seem very steady on his feet.

"Charlie was here?"

"Which bar are we at? We were in the Green Rooms and he was acting strangely…" Max was almost incoherent, the words coming out slurred. "Charlie isn't a bad guy, Will. He was bad to you, but he was jealous. I didn't think he would take it that far."

"Max, Charlie slept with my boyfriend in our bed and I caught them. I think he wanted to get caught."

"He misses you."

"I doubt that very much."

Max hung his head, all energy gone. "He's not the same anymore. He left me! He never would have left me before."

Irritation bloomed at my brother for leaving his friend like this, and I wondered what'd happened as getting this wasted was out of character for Max.

"Did you guys have a fight?"

"He's drinking too much, Will. I'm worried something is going to happen to him." Max covered his mouth with his hands and lurched away from me a bit.

"You gonna get sick?" He nodded. "Let's try some fresh air," I suggested, leading him towards the door. The crowd was thick around us and I had to push our way through. There was no way to get back to the others to say bye, so I decided to text them when I got outside instead.

Outside, Max leaned on the side of the building looking a rather alarming shade of green. A minute later, he threw up in the gutter. "Dammit, no way are you getting an Uber now."

When he finished, fresh tears appeared. "I'm sorry, Will! I ruined your night." Pity flared and I gave him a hug before towing him to my car.

"I'll take you home."

Twenty One - Andy

What. The. Actual. Fuck?! Did I just see Will take another guy home? I'd pushed through the crowded bar when I saw Will leaving, wondering what was going on. When I'd eventually gotten outside, I caught him hugging a little blonde guy before putting an arm around his shoulders and leading him away.

I stood dazed for awhile until I was jostled by a group of people leaving. Coming to my senses, I went back to the others. Something must have shown on my face because they all were concerned. "I think Will just took home a hookup!" I blurted out.

"No chance." "No!" "No way, there must be an explanation." The last one was Brad's voice of reason.

"When I got outside, he was hugging this blonde guy. Then he put his arm around him and they walked off together. That looks bad, right? I'm not just making something out of nothing?"

"Well, yes it does look bad, but if it's the same guy I saw him help, then he might just be a friend or something. The kid looked really out of it." Brad raised an eyebrow and carried on, "Will cares about you. He wouldn't do that, I'm sure of it. If it turns out that he did, then my friendship with him is over. I hope he's better than that."

A prickle of shame made its way through me. Why had I been so quick to think the worst of Will? It'd been my automatic thought. I needed to stop taking baggage from other relationships around. Of course there'd be a reasonable explanation for what I'd seen that didn't mean that Will was about to leap into bed with another guy. Not right after I'd confessed my feelings.

"Nah, you're right. There's a reason. I'll head on out now and call him when I get home." I got up to leave, dropping a kiss on Brad's cheek. "Thanks, Daddy Bear."

"No problem, Baby Bear. Get home safe, okay? And check in." The others waved and I left, relieved to be away from the tension surrounding them. I couldn't see Brad staying much longer either.

Not up to walking and unable to drink, I'd taken my car. Getting back to my apartment didn't take long, so I got ready for bed before calling Will. That part of me that was still doubting him didn't expect an answer, but after only a couple of rings he picked up.

"Hey, Andy. Shit! I was going to text. Are you still at the bar?" Smiling at the tinge of panic in his tone, I said, "No, I'm home now. Just wanted to see where you went. I, uh, saw you with that guy outside."

"Did you see Max throw up, too? Shit, that was nasty." I could hear the distaste in his voice and picture the wrinkle in his nose as he screwed up his face. "Thought he was going to puke in my car! His roommate wasn't impressed when I dropped him off." He chuckled. "Not my problem now, though. He's going to feel it tomorrow."

"Not going to lie, I, uh, thought he was maybe a hookup." I said hesitantly, wanting to be fully honest with Will. "Brad said there'd be an explanation. I feel really bad I jumped to the wrong conclusion. Only, I saw you hug him and put your arm around him....." My voice trailed off.

"I can see where you got that idea from, then," his tone was gentle, "Y'know I wouldn't do that to you right? Hell, I haven't even noticed another person that way since the day we met."

"Seriously?"

"Deadly serious. Even when you were shooting down my ideas and messing around with our desk."

I couldn't help but laugh.

"I'm getting my shit together, Andy. I want us to be together but I have a whole lot of hang ups, and I want to deal with them first, okay? Can you hold out a bit longer?"

"Absolutely."

Twenty Two - Andy

I woke up on Saturday with the biggest smile on my face. The call with Will had done a lot to really clear the air. He told me he was starting therapy for some of the issues he had with commitment and relationships. Knowing that he'd been badly hurt, I thought that it was a great idea. The therapy that I'd received from the group I went to had helped me out of a bad place when we lost mom, so I was a supporter of it. I was proud of him for making that decision, and told him so. His descriptions and stories of Dr. Arnold were hilarious. They really seemed to have bonded on their video call.

There wasn't much for me to do around the apartment and I realized I hadn't seen my sister in a while. She came over and brought lunch from the bakery on the corner, so she was officially my favorite person, at least until my jeans didn't fit properly any more.

Spending the day being coddled because of my leg wasn't a bad way to pass the time. Josh came over after soccer and made dinner for us all, distracting Abby when she got a little overbearing. I loved them dearly but it was a relief to have them out of my space.

Facing an interrogation squad was probably easier than dealing with Abby when she wanted to get info. I'd told her, with as few details as possible, about the cabin and my accident. We'd discussed the Henry and Gem situation a bit, as I tried to avoid all things Will-related. Without having anything else I wanted to share, because I was not telling her that I'd slept with Will again, I turned the focus onto her current projects.

One thing I'd neglected to tell Abby about was my haircut from the doctor at the clinic. Abby laughed until she cried over my mortification. I even caught Josh trying to cover his amusement over it.

Successfully managing to avoid talking about Will all day was a challenge. I barely mentioned sharing a room with him. I definitely didn't talk about sharing a bed, and Will looking after me became a group effort instead. Abby and Josh left and my secrets were intact.

I hated lying; even the omission felt like a lie, but it was going to take a lot for Abby to see Will in a good light. I had time to sort that out while he got himself together, though.

***

October melted into November and before I knew it, December was about to begin. Yet Will and I were stuck in a strange sort of holding pattern. Gone were the hangouts we enjoyed before the cabin trip. We were rarely alone together except at work where we couldn't really talk properly. Will would make excuses to leave if I caught him unexpectedly, or would invite other people to join us. Pete had ended up at a movie that I tried to turn into a date. Brad joined us for coffee. I soon got the message and only arranged group outings after that.

There was none of the casual intimacy that we shared before we slept together. Instead of moving forward in our relationship, we'd taken steps back. I'd thought it would take a couple of weeks, and then maybe we would go on some dates or something. Nothing like that happened, though.

Irritated and lonely, I'd tried calling Will to chat after a couple of weeks, but he was always too busy for me. My texts were replied to with a vague, "soon," or my favorite, "not yet." So, after a few weeks, I'd given up. I'd tried to keep him in my life but he seemed to be slipping away from me. It was a strange time for me. I stopped spending time with the guys from the gym too, since all they did was ask questions about what was going on with Will when he couldn't hear them.

The anniversary of my mom's accident hit me hard and other than a brief visit with my twin who was also struggling with her own grief, I spent it alone. I lit a candle for my mom and talked to her about all that had changed since the last anniversary.

Late that night as I was curled up in bed, I received a text from Will that helped, but was far from enough. I'd been drowning in grief all day on my own, not wanting to lean on Abby and Josh, and unable to reach out to the guys because of the recent distance. I wanted Will to give me more than what I'd got.

Will: Thinking of you today *heart emoji*

He'd apologized when I'd seen him in the office for not sending the text sooner and I'm sure he felt my frustration, though I muted most of my anger. A text wasn't what I'd wanted. I'd wanted the support of my friend, at the very least.

When Abby asked if anything was happening with Will at Thanksgiving dinner at her house, I'd been honest when I'd answered, "No, we're just friends." Though we were barely that at this point.

Despondent at the mention of Will, I'd missed the gleeful look on her face which soon slipped into something like concern. She shared a look with Josh but didn't question me deciding to leave their home early. Being around a happy couple was hard when that happiness seemed to have moved further out of reach for me.

The office was closed for a few days over Thanksgiving so that we could all spend time with our families. I couldn't spend all of it with Abby, even if Josh's parents had invited me over too. They were sweet people, but I just wanted to wallow. Instead, I spent that time alone, trying to cut those strings that kept Will tied in my heart.

Twenty Three - Andy

Abby called me the first Saturday of December, sounding far too cheerful for the early hour. If I'd dared call her at this time, I could guarantee that I would be chewed out for it, but hypocrisy, thy name was Abby.

"Hello, hello, little brother!" Not giving me time to reply, she carried on, "So, I have a favor to ask. Well, it isn't for me. It's for *someone I know well*." There was a strange stress on the last part. "They need to ask for a favor, but I'm sure you'll be up for it."

Grumbling, both at her all-too-chirpy tone and the early hour, as I'd been unable to sleep until really late and still woke with the dawn light. I managed, "What's the favor, Abs? It's too early for this shit, y'know?"

She cackled over the line, "Revenge for all those early calls you've given me." She paused for a long minute, making me pull the phone away from my ear to check that she hadn't muted me or put me on hold, since she'd done both before. She was quiet for a moment longer before she said in a more sober tone, "You can say no, okay? Jonas needs a date to a charity gala, tonight. He'd like to take you."

"What?" I shot up from the sofa and started pacing, "He's going to out himself officially? He's always kept away from discussions on his sexuality, I mean, I figured that if you were setting me up with him, he was at least bi, but...."

"Andy, chill out a sec. So, it's been rumored for ages that he's bisexual, and when I met him, I'd told him about you. I even showed him a picture on my phone. He said you were cute."

"Seriously?"

"Yeah, so I said that you'd be interested but were coming out of something. I may've mentioned after Thanksgiving that you were still single. He called me just now, asking if I would get you to call him, and to warn you that he wants to take you to this gala."

"Holy shit!"

Her laughter echoed in my ears as she disconnected the call and texted me his number. I was going to call Jonas Temper. He wanted to take me on a date! Somewhere we would be seen.

I paced for a little while longer to burn off some nervous energy and psych myself up for calling him. Deciding to send him a text first so that he had my number too, I almost dropped my phone when he called me instead.

"Andy," his rich voice held no accent, having likely been trained out of him.

"Hi," I squeaked, my throat closing with nerves. He laughed, which soothed me. "Hey," I tried again the word coming out normally this time, "Abby said something about a gala?"

"Yeah, listen, I know it's a big ask, but I need to go with someone and I finally feel ready to share that part of myself with the world. I've always wanted to do it on my terms, y'know what I mean?"

"I get that. I really do. Are you sure you want to do that with someone you haven't met yet?"

"This might sound weird, but I think it's safer this way. Say, for example, I was in a relationship, and the guy freaked out because he couldn't take the pressure of the limelight, that would ruin everything."

His words held a note of pain. There was more to this story, I was sure of that, but I wanted to meet him. Asking me to help him like this was an honor.

"Actually, I get that. I have to be honest. There's this guy….." I took the time to fill in this perfect stranger, the whole story of Will, and everything that I still had to tell my sister. When I was finished, I heard him sigh and thought for sure I'd ruined everything.

"You have no idea how much of a relief that is. I was going to ask if it could just be as friends. I know Abby wants this to be a proper date, and for us to really hit it off, but I have my own Will. He doesn't want to risk outing me, but doesn't want to live in the closet, so things are kinda off just now."

My heart hurt for Jonas, "Well, that's perfect then. I can handle a little heat for being your first guy date. Then your man will see it isn't a big deal, and that it won't ruin your career. Then you can start being seen with him in public." I tried to sound enthusiastic, but I was nervous. The idea of being in the limelight for this was scary, but I could handle that to allow Jonas to come out in his own way.

He laughed, clearly relieved, "Let's hope so. Maybe your man will get the hint that you aren't waiting around forever and do something. I'm so glad you're on board and I can be honest with you. I didn't want to give you the wrong impression."

"I'm glad I can help you out. How fancy is this gala? Because I have a decent suit, but not a tux." I began to stress out at finding a tux at this late stage. I didn't think I could afford to buy one, but I could rent a decent-fitting one, possibly.

"Abby has your measurements apparently, and is altering one my assistant is taking over. Then they will take it to you. I'll need your address for that, and for the limo to pick you up."

It all felt like something out of a fairytale, but at the same time there was a trickle of unease flowing through me.

As if sensing it, Jonas tried to ease my conscience. "You don't owe Will anything. Certainly not after weeks of radio silence on what's happening. You've asked, and he hasn't given you anything. You can't wait around forever. I think he needs to learn that." He paused for a moment. "For my own part, I'm going to message my own man and let him know you're a friend before he sees any photos."

I thought about warning Will, but decided not to. I didn't need to check with him that it was okay to go on a friend date. Sure, to the outside world it'd look like a proper date. If he was hurt by that, then maybe he could see that he had been hurting me with all these weeks of nothing.

"Yeah, you're right, it just feels weird. But we aren't on a romantic date. This is a friends thing, so, yeah..."

He let out another chuckle, "It'll be fine, Andy. If not, you get a new friend, a nice evening out, and a perfectly tailored tux." The laughter vanished from his voice. "Time to show Will what he's missing out on."

Twenty Four - Will

Far too early on Sunday morning my phone ringing woke me from the little sleep I'd managed to get. I was sure I'd set it to do not disturb, but lack of sleep had left my brain foggy. It took me a minute to realize that if it was ringing, then it was important. A strange foreboding feeling played over me when I saw it was my mom.

"Hey Mom, everything okay?"

"Will," came her frantic voice, I could hear panicked breaths, "have you seen Alex?" a lead weight settled in my chest. Alex. Of course it was about Alex.

"What's going on?" I asked hesitantly. I was supposed to be arranging to meet with him as part of my therapy, but kept putting it off, reluctant to spend any time with him. Dr. Arnold had been incredibly patient with me, but I could see that it was beginning to wear thin.

"He's left Helena and Joseph. She gave him some news yesterday and he just left. He didn't come home last night. I don't know where he is and he won't answer his phone for me." Everything seemed to stop. I couldn't hear the traffic outside; I didn't seem to be breathing.

"What?" I gasped out before pure rage filled me. How could he? After everything he had put me through for Helena, how could he just up and leave her? It didn't make any sense.

Distantly, I could hear Mom talking about them having troubles, trying counseling, something about a separation, but it didn't really register. "Mom," I interrupted, "I'll call some people and see if I can find him. Could you send me his number? I don't have it anymore. Not since I changed mine." I paused to get myself together. "What do you want me to say to him?" I took a deep breath; this last question was so difficult for me to ask. "Do you want him to go back to her?"

I could hear her crying quietly, probably trying to muffle the noise so she could keep it from me. "No," she managed to get out, "I think it's best that they are done." A sniff, then, "I think there's some things you need to know, but maybe they need to come from your brother. Do you think there is any chance you would hear him out?" Her tone was gentle, but I could feel how desperately she wanted this from me. The last five years with things as they were with us had been hard on mom and my little sister, Matilda.

I sighed, "I dunno, Mom," was my honest answer. Maybe it was time to clear the air with Alex; Dr. Arnold certainly thought so. There was nothing between Helena and I except hurt feelings now. I'm not sure I ever really loved her in the way I was supposed to, but I'd been about to marry her, and she'd broken my heart. That, and ruined my relationship with my brother forever. I just wasn't sure if I wanted my brother in my life after what they had put me through. Either of my brothers, since they'd both betrayed me.

I got off the phone after assuring her there were people that Alex used to be in contact with that he might go to. She'd already tried his most recent friends before calling me, showing that she was really worried if she thought that Alex would come here. The guy had plenty of money, he could've taken a vacation for all I knew, but mom had said that Helena had his passport so he hadn't left the country.

Why they were making so much of it, I didn't know. Not until I had called Christian, who had been Alex's best friend up until he suddenly married my fiancée. I'd been both shocked and touched that Christian had come down on my side of things, and we had kept in touch ever since. At one point I'd considered him one of my closest friends.

Christian had always been one of those guys that didn't repeat gossip. He hated liars and cheats. He didn't exaggerate. If he told you something, it was a true fact. So when he told me that my brother had been having mental health issues, and had possibly had some sort of breakdown, I'd been floored. I spent so long unable to speak that Christian thought the call had dropped and he'd called me back.

Alex had gone to Christian over a year ago to make amends. Christian had always looked up to Alex, with the way he looked after us with our father often being absent from our lives. So he'd taken it hard when it turned out that Alex and Helena had betrayed me so horribly. Christian couldn't understand how my apparently loving brother had done me so wrong. He and Alex had a massive argument over it and hadn't spoken until Alex appeared at Christian's door asking for help putting things right.

Father had been proud of Alex for taking what he wanted, and for a long time I avoided my father, horrified that he could applaud one son for ruining the life of another. Hadn't my happiness meant anything to him? Charlie seemed to think this was something to copy, the little piece of shit. Mom had been torn between warring sons, but thankfully

Matilda, who had only been thirteen at the time, was kept from most of it. I'd cut off half of my family for my sanity.

Christian had appeared at the place I'd shared with Helena a week after their announcement and helped me pick up the pieces. In some ways Christian had replaced Alex as the man that I looked up to.

We talked for awhile and for the first time in a long time I found myself opening up. In truth, I'd been avoiding calling or meeting up with Christian since stuff had started with Andy, for fear of his judgment. Now though, I told him about Andy, how I'd kept him at length because nothing good in my life was permanent. About therapy, and how much I had missed my brother. He had laughed when I'd clarified I'd meant Alex, not Charlie. That one could eat shit.

Hearing that Alex had been struggling with his guilt, about the realities of a life with Helena made me feel sorry for him. There was still anger there for sure. Deep down, I knew I'd never fully forgive him. Never properly trust him, but was there a part of me that could put it aside? Maybe have Alex in my life again?

Our call was interrupted by the front desk calling. Christian hung up after assuring me I'd be the first to hear if Alex appeared.

"Mr. Petraki? There is another Mr. Petraki here, saying he's your brother and asking if he could come up. Shall I put him on the list?" Earl, the desk attendant asked.

"Could you ask if it's Alex or Charlie, please?"

"One moment sir," there were a few seconds of hold music before "Alex, sir."

"Let him up and put him on the list."

"Of course, sir."

I thanked Earl and quickly went to straighten up and text Mom that Alex was here. She must have been holding her phone, because she tried to call immediately, but I sent the call to voicemail. Quickly texting back that I'd call when Alex had left, I told her that I'd talk to him and see if I could help him or convince him to go to her place.

I didn't say he didn't deserve any kindness from me but that I was willing to hear him out. Therapy must be working because I was curious about how it all happened, how long it'd been going on.

Alex rang the bell and when I opened the door it was to a man that was a shadow of his former self. He was thin, in a hollow sort of way, like the life had just drained out of him. Stress had aged him; the hair around his temples more grey than our shared dark chocolate brown. There were fine lines around his eyes and some crinkling around his forehead. I don't think I'd seen him in jeans and a t-shirt in about a decade, and both were crumpled, like he'd slept in them.

I stepped back to let him in and headed to the kitchen to make some coffee and maybe find some snacks, with Alex trailing behind me silently.

He remained quiet, hovering in the doorway as I moved around the room, keeping myself busy and pushing down conflicting feelings of pity and rage. I served us up coffee and gestured to the table, realizing that neither of us had spoken yet.

We sat at the breakfast table in the corner of the kitchen in tense silence, each holding our oversize mugs as if they would defend us from this conversation. Minutes passed as we sat studying each other before Alex dropped his eyes to the table and seemed to shrink further into himself for a minute. Taking a breath he looked up with a new sort of resolve in his eyes, blue like Mom's.

"I'm so sorry, Wilbert," his voice so soft and filled with regret as he used his old nickname for me. My heart cracked when I saw a tear slip from his red-rimmed eyes. I'd never seen him cry before. I thought he couldn't cry. He hadn't at Father's funeral.

He wiped the tear away roughly. "I have no excuse for what we did to you. It might not seem like it now, but I truly did love Helena. I thought she loved me too, but as hard as we tried, we just didn't work out." He let out a dark chuckle, devoid of any real humor. "What we had started out in deception, so it had no real foundation. We did all we could, but what we shared, it wasn't love. It was lust. We got sucked into this thing that just…snowballed into something else."

He looked at me before dropping his eyes. He must have seen something in my expression though, because he continued.

"When I first met Helena, you'd taken her to brunch with the family and I remember thinking how gorgeous she was. You were announcing the engagement. I think you said you'd been together a little while."

I nodded at him. "Nearly a year, but I'd put off meeting the family because of Father, mostly."

"You two seemed to fit and it just worked, y'know?" She seemed so happy and like she wanted to be a part of the family. I don't think you heard but Father made a few comments about her background. About coming from a single parent family, just wanting you for your money, that kinda thing. Helena heard and seemed really embarrassed about it, so I spoke up for her. I made a point to chat to her, and from then on she kinda latched onto me. I wanted to get to know her because she seemed important to you, not because she was pretty.

"Turns out Christian was dating her best friend so we met up a couple of times as a group, and sometimes Chris and Lacey would vanish. At first it was really awkward, we didn't know what to say to each other, but I guess we became friends. You were always at work, so I guess she never told you about it."

I thought back to that time, full of late night client meetings and dinners. Sometimes I would invite Helena, but more often than not she made excuses. Often because she had dinner or drinks plans with friends. Overworked, I hadn't questioned anything. Like why my fiancée hardly spent time with me, even when we shared an apartment.

"It was months later and Lacey and Chris had broken up, but Helena and I were good friends by then and still saw each other often. She told me that you guys were having problems. Fighting about planning the wedding." He stalled then, fresh tears in his eyes. His expression was tortured. "I'd fallen in love with her by then. I hadn't told anyone, because Chris would've been furious with me, but I'd promised myself I wouldn't do anything about it."

He looked so earnest that I couldn't help but feel sorry for him, but then I remembered he'd acted on his feelings. Clearly seeing my expression harden with anger he carried on hurriedly, "There was one night, a couple of months before that last big work trip you went on. I'd been out drinking with some people from the office. We bumped into you guys. D'you remember?"

He looked at me and I nodded, recalling the night and the argument that followed. I'd always wondered why Helena had picked that fight.

"So, I'd just gotten home, a bit worse for wear. When she called me crying, I asked her to come over to my place since I wasn't fit to drive and she was already in an Uber. I'm not going to excuse my actions for what happened after. We had sex and she stayed the night. I remember the guilt killing me in the morning when you called, and she lied saying that she stayed at Lacey's. It felt like a punch to the gut. I'd betrayed you, and she had lied so casually about it. You guys made up and we agreed that it was a one-off. It wouldn't happen again."

He stopped to look at me to make sure I knew he was being truthful, "And it didn't until after you had gone off on that trip for work. The London office, I think. You were gone for, what? Three, four months? I'm not making any excuses here. Helena called about a week or so after you left, crying and saying how she had made a mistake saying yes to you. That she should have ended it after we'd slept together. She asked me to come over. I knew it was a mistake before I even went."

I had to stop him there, "You still went, though," I gritted out, anger at the depth of the betrayal getting the best of me.

Alex put his head in his hands. "I'm so sorry!" he whispered.

"I just need a second," I told him and I fled from the room.

Hiding out in the bathroom, I took my phone from my pocket and texted Christian. I thought about texting Andy, but over the last couple of weeks things had been strained between us. I'd asked for space but instead had created a gulf between us. Plus, Chris knew Alex and all that had happened.

Will: Alex is here. He's telling me everything. He looks so broken, but I'm still so angry! What should I do?

Not expecting an immediate reply, I startled when it buzzed in my hand and I dropped the phone into the thankfully empty sink.

Christian: It all depends if you think you can forgive him. Has he told you why they broke up? He hasn't gone into details, but I know they've been having problems for a while. They've had a trial separation for a bit, too. I think he's always felt guilty over how they started out.

Considering this for a minute, I figured I'd better hear Alex out. I couldn't decide on where we went from here without listening to it all. Once I'd done that I could then decide how I felt, and where we went from there.

Will: No, not all. Just up until after I went away for work to London. Gonna hear him out. Thanks for being there for me. Do you want me to send him round later?

Christian: Just see how it goes. Message me later. Tell him he can stay here with us if he needs to. Naomi won't mind.

Putting my phone away, I returned to the kitchen. My brother was sitting and looking out of the window, clearly deep in thought. I was still furious, feeling betrayed at what they had done. There was a part of me that hurt to see the brother that I'd always admired, aspired to be like, looking so thoroughly wrecked.

I sat at the table. "Just get it all out. I'll try not to interrupt you again," I told him plainly.

"Will…." his voice broke on my name and I knew then that it didn't matter what he'd done. My brother was broken and needed me to fix him. He sniffed and looked like he was working out how to continue before I stopped him.

"When did you last sleep?"

"I….I think yesterday I got a couple of hours, maybe?"

I got up. "Come with me." and I felt him follow me through the apartment to the bedrooms. "This is my room, but this one here - " I motioned across the hall from the master, "is a spare. There's fresh sheets and it has its own half bath." He looked at me in confusion. "Get a shower, have a nap and we can talk after. I'll bring you some sweats to sleep in." In his current state, I thought my things would actually be loose on him. We had always been the same size, more like twins even with the two years separating us. All he could do was nod quietly, thank me and head into his room to rest.

Back in the kitchen I thought about what Alex had told me. Part of me was relieved that not all of my relationship with Helena had been lies. They hadn't had a thing for more than a few months really before it'd all come out. It still stung, but it was a distant pain. I think it had made it easier to deal with that they had gotten married and had Joey. Unlike what'd happened with Charlie and Ethan. Charlie had thrown Ethan away after they'd gotten caught, the thrill of getting one over on me gone, and so was the interest in my boyfriend.

Alex and Helena though, they hadn't just been a fling, but something real. I think that was why I couldn't wrap my head around the fact that Alex had left her. Something really bad must've happened for him to do that. I'd seen photos and videos of their life together, I couldn't avoid it as Mom wanted me to know my nephew, and they'd seemed so in love. Had it all been an act? Why, though?

After pottering around in the kitchen for a bit, I heard the shower shut off and the sounds of Alex moving around the spare room. When the sounds stopped and I realized I was just standing in a quiet apartment, I knew I had to get out for a bit. Leaving a note on the coffeemaker for Alex, I grabbed my things and headed for the gym.

***

I knew I was avoiding thinking about Alex and Helena and all the revelations there, but I knew there were more to come and was trying to brace myself for the worst. I was also thinking about Andy and all the things that I'd told Christian about him while I lifted weights.

Henry was working on the main floor rather than reception today. It was a relief to see him in a good mood. His break up with Gem was well and truly over and done with. I'd seen a new lightness in him as he walked the gym floor chatting to people. Before he noticed me at least. He visibly tensed as he approached me.

"Hey, man. How are you?" There was a strange note of pity in his voice that I didn't understand.

"I'm alright, needing to blow off some steam, though. How's it going?"

He tensed, "Andy?"

"Andy? Nothing's wrong there as far as I know. Just dealing with my brother. He's at my apartment and I need to work out some stuff."

"So you haven't spoken to Andy today, or heard anything about him?" he questioned looking wary.

"Nope, I woke up to family drama. I haven't seen him since the office on Friday. He had dinner with Abby that night."

"Fuck."

Resting the weight and sitting up so I could talk to Henry properly, I was alarmed at the expression on his face. He looked like he wanted to flee from this situation; literally be doing anything other than dropping the bomb he was about to land in my lap.

"Look…Shit. Hold on, I need my phone. I think it's better you just see rather than me telling you."

I was left sweating, fearing that something truly awful had happened to Andy. I was ready to get up and run to the locker room so I could call him to see if he was okay. Though it was doubtful he would pick up after I'd ignored all his calls.

The minutes that passed felt like years as I watched Henry go to reception to get his phone and have a whispered conversation with his sister. They both glanced at me, looking worried before catching me staring and looking away.

Henry walked back to me like he was about to face his execution. "Okay, so don't shoot the messenger. I had no idea about this. No one did."

He passed me his phone with an article loaded on the main screen. Reading the headline, my heart seized in my chest. *"Jonas Temper brings mystery man to gay charity gala."*

Scanning the page, I thought I was going to vomit when the actor was pictured with his arm around my Andy, the two of them sharing a joke. The piece told me that they'd turned up to a LGBTQA+ charity gala, finally silencing the debate on Jonas's sexuality.

Jonas was even quoted! *"I wanted to confirm that I'm bisexual on my own terms and I'm so happy that Andy could be here to support me. As a gay man, he understands how difficult coming out can be. Doing it while supporting this worthy charity made sense."*

There were so many pictures of them, including one that Andy had shared on his Instagram with them obviously in the limo before the event. Their heads together, holding half-full champagne glasses with the hashtags #myhero and #proud as well as the tags for the charity.

Emotions rose in me, shocking in their intensity. I hated that man! Jonas. He had taken Andy from me. I wanted to be sick, but I had to push the feelings down. This was all my own fault.

How many times was he supposed to hear "soon" before giving up? I'd felt it in all of our interactions recently. The distance spanning between us had grown to the point that our friends would cast uneasy glances at each other when we were all together. Not that it'd happened often lately. Fuck! I'd made such a mess of things! Brushed him off, too consumed with my plan of action instead of talking to Andy.

"Will." Henry's voice pulled me out of my spinning thoughts and he placed a hand on my shoulder as the other eased his phone from my hand carefully. "Are you okay?"

"Honestly? I don't know. One thing that I do know is that this is my fault. Andy hasn't done anything wrong. I've been unfair to him, keeping him hanging." I hung my head. I felt gutted and could only blame myself.

I got up, deciding to go. There were important things to do and hiding at the gym wouldn't fix the mess I'd made of the first real thing I could've had. First there was my brother and then Andy. Maybe if I could get closure with the Alex and Helena thing, I could stop being half in, and give Andy everything he deserved.

***

After leaving the gym, I wandered around for a while, just lost in thought and trying to come to terms with the idea of Andy dating someone that wasn't me. That feeling of nausea reared again.

182

How had we gotten here? He'd been so patient. Andy had tried to talk to me so many times and I'd brushed him off. He'd taken all my shit and I'd treated him like a fucking doormat.

Without thinking about it, I somehow ended up outside of his apartment. A place I knew I had no business being knowing that I had nothing to offer him yet. Or even if he wanted anything to do with me at all. Maybe he'd be better off with the actor. If he could be happy with that guy, then would I accept that and move on? I'd like to think that I cared about him enough that I could.

Hell, I more than cared about him. He was my best friend and lover. The one that made me smile. Made me want to be a better person. For him, I'd do anything. I loved everything about him. I loved him, and his happiness was worth everything. I don't know when it had happened, probably when we truly became friends and I'd let him see the real me. I'd fallen in love with Andy, and then I'd broken his heart. His pulling away was him protecting himself from his hurt.

Turning away without going to see him was the hardest thing I'd ever done. I wanted to pour my heart out to him and confess my feelings, but I knew he had to see how sorry I was first. I had to play the long game here. Eventually he would see that this guy wasn't for him and I'd be ready. I'd have my shit together and show him I was all in. I wanted it all. Him in my bed, or me in his since his apartment actually felt like a home, all the time. Boyfriends. Holidays with family. A cat. Hell, a dog if he wanted. I could see us married someday. I wanted a future with him.

Twenty Five - Will

Alex was on the couch when I got home. He looked refreshed, but still gaunt. His dark circles were less apparent and he was now freshly shaven. I was pleased to see that he was eating, having clearly ordered some takeout while I was gone since I doubted there was much food in the fridge.

Dressed in some sweats that I'd left for him and an old stretched out t-shirt, he looked vulnerable in a way he never had before. More real. Not like the man I had placed up on a pedestal.

Breaking the silence, I asked "Did you get much sleep?" He glanced up at me, taking his attention off the news that was playing on low on the TV while he picked at his food, appetite clearly gone.

"An hour or so. You've been gone a while. Everything okay?"

I was tempted to play it off as nothing but honestly, where would that get us? Alex was here with his marriage apparently in tatters and he'd been opening up to me about what had happened. Something that five years later I still didn't understand.

When I had asked why before, back when it all had happened, I was told to let it go. Like anyone could just "let it go" if the person that they thought they were going to marry just, all of a sudden, ended up married to someone else. Someone who happened to be their brother.

Father had insisted that Helena not be put under any stress for fear of anything happening to the baby. For him, it was all about the baby. His heir was having an heir and the rest of us might as well not exist.

I'd been too angry to speak to Alex, more heartbroken by his actions than hers. If he'd been just a random guy then it would have been easier to take because looking back, I wasn't as in love with her as I should've been with our wedding only months away. Not that it made it right, just easier to cope with. Like I'd escaped making a big mistake. I was more hurt by his betrayal.

Though, I did wonder if I only felt that way knowing how differently I felt about Andy. What I had with him, even as dysfunctional as it was, eclipsed what I'd felt for Helena.

Getting an explanation from any source in my family was impossible. Aside from Father's funeral, that welcome home dinner had been the last time that we were all in one place together. Even when he had the heart attack months before he died, we took turns visiting him in the hospital. I had only gone once, still furious. Then he'd died and I had never fully forgiven my family for being on the other side of the line I'd drawn in the sand that day.

"I messed up," I admitted to him and he looked sad, like he knew that some of it was because of how he and his wife had treated me. "Yeah, me too Wilbert, me too," and I could see tears threaten to spill down those too-thin cheeks. So I did the only thing that I could think of. I sat next to my brother and pulled him into a hug and cried with him for a while.

I don't know how much time passed before we broke apart and tried to dry our eyes, but it'd been needed. It was cathartic to let the tears flow, to try and let go of the mistakes we had made.

"The reason Helena and I are through is more to do with how we started than anything else. It's always been there in our marriage. The guilt. It was like it tainted everything we had and it got to me. We should never have slept together that first time and it was inexcusable that we went behind your back when you were away. I should've pushed Helena to call you and end it. I don't know why she didn't say something and I know she had plenty of chances. I think part of her loved the drama and the sneaking about. But I let her, and that's on me too."

I wanted to interrupt him but I knew he needed to get this all out. "A month before you were due to come home from that trip, Helena came to my apartment upset. You'd been away just over two months at the time and you'd been fighting and um….hadn't had sex for a couple of weeks before that. So when she dropped the bomb that she was pregnant, I knew it had to be mine. We hadn't been using condoms because she was on the pill. Stupid, I know, but it happened. I still wonder if she stopped taking it. A week later I went with her to the doctor's appointment and she had a scan. There he was, on the screen. I loved him straight away. I didn't know then it was a boy, and it didn't matter to me like it did to Father. He was mine. There was no way he was yours. So even when I felt this utter joy that I was going to be a dad, I had this shard of pain in my chest because of what it was going to do to you.

"Helena didn't want to call you with the news. She wanted to break it to you in person but Father found out that I had left the office and when he found out why, he insisted I marry Helena immediately. He called her mom and between them, they booked a wedding for the week before you returned. It didn't matter that I wasn't sure if we were ready to be married.

"The wedding was small, rushed and unromantic. I knew I was making a mistake right then. Whatever I had with Helena wasn't strong enough to overcome the bad start we had. That dinner was a nightmare and I would've let you punch me if you'd gotten closer.

"We tried after that to work as a couple, to be good parents to Joe. Stuff always got in the way of us making a true go of it. Helena's mom split from one of her boyfriends and stayed with us for months. Then Father was ill and died and all the excuses for us to stay together seemed to vanish one by one."

He stopped then, seeming to run out of steam.

"You want a drink?" I asked him and he gave me a yes in reply. Getting up to head to the kitchen, I decided I wanted something stronger than water.

We talked for hours about the ups and downs of their marriage and as the hours passed, it became easier for me to deal with. The pain became distant. The trust between us might never be the same, but I could move on from this. Finally.

Alex had been forced into a corner by his own weakness. He had never stood up to Helena or my father and he'd suffered for that. Their marriage never stood a chance of surviving the pressure of tearing apart our family.

They'd been separated for a couple of months, but Alex had left their home when Helena announced that she was pregnant by her new boyfriend. Seeing that there was no way to rescue their marriage had broken him. He confessed to not being sure if he loved her, or the idea of her.

He had money and could go stay with Mom, but after my own epic fuckup with Andy, I was feeling charitable to my brother and asked if he would like to stay with me. I had the room and having someone to come home to would ease the loneliness I often felt. Mom burst into tears when I called her to assure her Alex was okay and tell her that he was staying with me.

Mom begged me to consider speaking to Charlie, but I'd reached my limit for now. I did tell her about what had happened with Max a few weeks ago at the bar. It kept popping into my mind at strange times. Charlie loved Max, and there was no way he'd just up and leave him somewhere, especially when Max was so vulnerable. I'd settle things with Alex and hopefully Andy, then get Dr. Arnold's support and advice on what to do about Charlie.

Alex called and had a short, terse, conversation with his soon to be ex-wife. He assured her he was fine and would visit his son soon and collect his things.

I told him all about Andy. Including details that I hadn't told Christian, like his confession to me the night we made love and my reaction. I poured my heart out to my brother and he listened quietly.

Alex cringed when I told him about pushing Andy away after promising to fix things and he held me as I cried when I broke down over Andy dating someone else.

We ordered more food later, because half a bottle of whiskey gone on an empty stomach was a bad idea. Drunk, we cleared the air as much as we could and likely forgot most of what was said.

Having Alex around wasn't quite the same as it was before. It never would be, but Andy wasn't Helena and I'd been looking at this all wrong. He should have been here with me as I helped my brother start to heal. Andy would've given me his love and support to allow me to help my family. I'd been so stupid and may have missed my chance with the best thing to ever happen to me.

Twenty Six - Andy

I'd been woken several times throughout the night into Sunday by my phone ringing and vibrating with messages on the nightstand. Frustrated and a little tipsy from all the champagne at the gala, I'd eventually switched my phone off.

Getting up after only a couple of hours of sleep was hard. My head hurt and my throat was dry, but I didn't want to lounge in bed all day. I knew that I'd have to turn my phone on soon, but I wanted to ignore reality for a while longer.

The gala had been a great experience. I smiled at the memories of the night as I hung up the beautifully made tux that I'd lain over the back of the sofa. The people had been welcoming and warm, the atmosphere hopeful as donations came rushing in. I'd placed some small bids on things like spa packages and other items that I thought Abby would appreciate if I won them.

Her Christmas gift was going to be the photo shoot I won for her. The photographer offered to take photos of Abby's designs and tailoring for her online store to help her grow her business. She could have a couples shoot if she wanted, though.

After hanging up my tux, showering and eating breakfast, I bit the bullet and turned on my phone.

Notification after notification flooded in and I regretted breakfast. Scanning through the messages, I was relieved that the press hadn't gotten my number or email address yet. It was unlikely that they were going to ignore me forever, but I could have hope that would be the case.

Most of the messages were from my sister. Compliments on how Jonas and I looked together and comments on how positively the press were reporting the gala. She asked if we'd hit it off and if there would be any more dates. I really didn't want to burst that bubble, but even if Jonas and I hadn't both been hung up on other people, I didn't think we were compatible.

I'd worried that the focus would be off the charity but Jonas had assured me that he'd warned them and that it'd raise their profile. He'd also given a significant donation, just in case.

Jonas had been great and I really hoped that he got his guy. I wasn't sure what would happen with mine. I knew that he didn't use social media, having deleted his profiles years ago.

As I sat pondering the situation, messages came in from Henry, Pete and Brad. All variations of, "What the fuck?" They couldn't have missed how strained it was between Will and I recently. I'd taken to reducing the amounts of time I spent with Will in a subtle way. At first I had started doing shorter, more frequent workouts, then I made excuses not to go to the bar or meet up on the weekends. It just made it easier, but I missed spending time with my friends.

I didn't reply to the guys. I felt bad about that, but I just wanted Will's reaction. Once I told them there was nothing in it, that it wasn't a real date, there was a risk that they'd tell him that. As petty as the whole thing was, I wanted to be the one to reassure him. I wanted him to come to me for answers.

Last night had given me a taste of an easier life, of dates and fun, easy conversation and uncomplicated affection. A taste of exactly what I wanted for myself.

Now I had to decide if I wanted Will to fight for what we could have, or if I wanted to give it up for good.

***

When I didn't hear from him all day, even after a message from Henry saying that Will knew, I kind of shut down a little. I don't know what I expected, but this silence wasn't it and it broke something inside me.

Hiding in bed, phone on mute, I passed the night tossing and turning, not really getting any real rest until exhaustion and sadness pulled me into sleep.

While I didn't wake up properly rested, I at least didn't look as awful as I felt. Getting ready for work on autopilot, I tried to stop obsessively checking my phone. Putting on the radio to cover the silence, I made the mistake of tuning in just as the entertainment news came on.

The news was still filled with stories about me and Jonas, but it seemed aside from my first name, there wasn't much information on me. The focus was more on the discussion about actors taking charge of how their personal lives are shown in the media.

It was a relief to get into the office and to try and focus on the campaigns that we were about to run. I spotted a couple of questioning glances and fully expected questions from Clara. I shut her down before she could ask, telling her that Jonas and I were friends and that he knew my sister. There was a part of me that wanted to hold that information back, but since Will knew and still hadn't said anything, or even approached me, then there was no point in hiding the truth.

I obviously was giving off a "don't fuck with me" vibe because I was able just to concentrate on my work rather than having to answer questions all day. While useful for work, it was lonely. I had several messages from Jonas, checking that I was okay and one with a picture of him and his man. In it, Jonas was pressing a kiss to the other guy's cheek. Both were smiling, so it seemed our plan worked out for him at least.

There were a number of times throughout the day that I spotted Will watching me, a look of sadness on his face that was quickly hidden if he noticed anyone watching him. He looked rough, like he was hungover, and spent a lot of the day on his phone.

We didn't talk about anything that wasn't work related and it seemed that we were both trying not to even need to do that either. I caught myself wanting to cry at how things had turned out. So much for soon, or for being his number one.

Twenty Seven - Will

I'd taken Clara aside to get the gossip on the date and almost fell to my knees with relief when she revealed that they'd just gone as friends. There was still a chance that I could fix this with Andy.

Over my lunch break, I took the time to really think through what I could do to turn this situation around. First things first though, I needed to apologize for pulling away and leaving him waiting.

My brother thought that perhaps this date had been Andy's way of showing me that he wasn't going to wait around forever. Why else would it be so public? It felt strange to be taking advice from my brother again, but it also gave me a warm feeling. Having Alex back in my life was going to be an adjustment. We weren't the same people we used to be.

Dr. Arnold was going to be impressed by my progress after weeks of stalling. We'd talked in circles in our sessions, and yes, it'd been helpful to have someone to listen to me, but it didn't get anyone anywhere.

To finally move forward with Andy, I had to give him what he said he wanted. Andy wanted dates, family, and friends. To be shown that he mattered and that I respected him and cared for him. So that was what he was going to get. If Jonas truly wasn't competition like Clara had said, then I was going to show him what he really meant to me.

Sending Dr. Arnold an email to follow up on my canceling my regular session, I outlined my weekend of revelations. Then I ordered some flowers for Andy and booked a nice restaurant for the following evening. Nothing too fancy, I knew

Andy wouldn't appreciate that. He liked good food, not when places tried too hard.

After work and picking up the flowers, I looked for some decent paper or a card so I could write what I was feeling. I'd always found it easier to write what I felt rather than say the words. They always got tangled and came out wrong.

I'd taken to carrying around my sketchbook and carefully tore out a drawing I'd done of Andy when we'd been at the cabin. During the first hike we'd taken a fair amount of breaks, and on one of those I took the time to watch Andy with the others. My pencil had flown over the paper almost without thought.

There was something in the expression in the drawing that was quintessentially Andy and I loved the picture. Often, I'd find myself flicking through the book just to look at it.

I carefully folded it into the simple card I'd chosen, just a heart on a plain cream background, and hoped that my words would heal this rift between us.

Approaching his building, I discovered that there was a problem. I had no way of getting this to his door. Calling Alex for advice helped; he suggested that I contact Andy's neighbor.

Bribing his neighbor twenty dollars to buzz me in and collect the bouquet and card from the elevator was the easiest solution. If I went to Andy's door myself, he might not answer. Same if I tried calling him.

Not that I hadn't thought of just calling him. I had. Every second since I'd heard about the date, but to me that was the simple way. I wanted to show Andy that he was worth the time and the effort that was needed to do this properly.

Message sent with the flowers and my note, and now I just had to wait and see if he accepted my dinner invitation.

***

It was strange to come home to someone there. Not only that, but a home-cooked meal. I wasn't the best cook, but I got by. Quite often I relied on store-bought meals or takeout, so home cooking was a real treat.

Over the space of a day, Alex had transformed in front of me. Gone was the haggard, almost frail, man. He was obviously still thin, but he held himself straight, no longer hunched and heavy with what must've been pain and shame. He'd shaved again and his blue eyes twinkled with joy.

"Hey, I hope it's okay, but Helena said I could have Joe for a couple of hours and give him dinner before dropping him off and picking up some more of my stuff."

So that was the reason for his happiness. "Of course, I've missed him. Where is he?"

I heard feet scampering over the hardwood floors from the corridor where the third bedroom that I'd made into an office was.

"Uncle Will! I made you a drawing. Daddy said I could use some paper and draw while he made dinner." My nephew held out his picture to me. In it I could see a couple of smudgy people, that I

196

assumed were Joseph and his daddy, next to what looked like a dinosaur.

"Is that a dinosaur?" I asked with wonder in my voice. For a four-year-old, it was a pretty good drawing and I wanted Joe to always have someone encouraging him, no matter what he decided to do, unless it was unsafe of course. I was a good uncle, not irresponsible.

Joe lit up with a beaming smile and I thanked my mother for making sure that I saw my nephew often enough that he knew me and felt comfortable around me.

I knelt to be more on his level and praised his drawing and listened to him explain it to me. Looking up, I saw Alex watching us with a soft look, his eyes glistening like tears were ready to drop, but he took a deep breath and pushed them back.

"Dinner's ready. Joe, wash your hands first, please." Alex commanded in a gentle tone.

"Okay, Daddy." Joe left me holding his picture and dashed off towards the bathroom without question.

"You sure this is okay?" Alex asked.

"Absolutely. Actually I think it's a great distraction from waiting to hear back from Andy." I said firmly as I leaned in the doorway watching my brother finish up dinner.

"So you went with the flowers and note?"

Alex began plating up our food, already far more comfortable in my apartment than I'd ever been. I didn't have it in me to resent him for that either. My apartment felt better for having him here.

We ate together at the table with Joe perched on his dad's knee since there were only two seats.

"I'm going to order a bigger table and more chairs this weekend for sure," I told Alex. Turning to Joe I asked, "What do you think, Joe? At least four seats, right?"

He nodded and started counting off on his fingers. "A chair for me, Daddy, Uncle Will, Mommy, Craig and the new baby. So this many!" he said, holding up his small hands with the incorrect number of fingers down.

My heart sank, worried at Alex's response to Joe casually putting us all together. Not to mention that it was far too soon for me to see Helena. Alex though, just chuckled.

"You forgot Andy, little dude." He said grinning at me.

"Who's Andy, Daddy?" The poor kid looked confused.

"Uncle Will's boyfriend, buddy."

Joe just shrugged, "Okay, a chair for Uncle Andy too then. Can I sleep here soon?" He asked to leave the table before we could respond, desperate to make another drawing before he had to go home. I stopped him as he passed to give him a quick hug and to drop a kiss on his head.

My eyes burned at how casually Joe added Andy into his family circle and Alex squeezed my shoulder as he got up to start on the dishes. Seeing that I needed to get myself together, he put on some music and sang tunelessly as he washed up.

As I sat processing the last couple of days my phone buzzed in my pocket. I'd tried to ignore it all night, but I'd been constantly aware of it.

One line of text showed when I lit the screen up.

Andy: Yes to dinner. Last chance.

There was no stopping the tear that slipped free. Alex must've heard some sort of noise escape me as he turned, and seeing my face, immediately got the wrong impression.

"Oh, Will," he started to say.

"I've got one last chance."

Twenty Eight - Andy

After a strange day, it was almost a relief to go home to the emptiness and silence of my apartment.

Thanks to Clara, I hadn't had to answer many questions about my non-date date at the gala. I couldn't figure out if that was a relief or not since there'd been no reaction from Will.

Let's face it, the only reason I'd gone through with it was to get some attention from the man, but still…nothing. Frustrated and hurt, I was tempted to go do something stupid. Like sign up for online dating, or go to a bar. I'd likely just buy myself a new toy online. Something I'd been eyeing for a while, like the tentacle dildo I'd never removed from my basket.

Getting home soaked and freezing from the downpour outside was the topping on the shit sundae of my day. I'd stomped off to the shower, complaining the whole time about my car refusing to start and having to leave it at work. I'd left work too late to deal with it today, and the office had been empty by the time I'd gotten out of my last video conference so no one could give me a ride home. The cleaners had neatly piled all my things on my desk which had been the only nice thing to happen.

Tired, grumpy and just plain lonely, I ordered some food even though I wasn't in the slightest bit hungry.

The door buzzed not long after. Confused as it was too soon to be my food, I opened the door to my neighbor from 5A. He was a young guy, a student at the university, and our paths had crossed a few times with mail being mixed up. Thankfully, he'd never gotten any of my packages.

Taylor was holding a large bouquet of sunflowers and pale roses and held them out to me.

"I was asked to give these to you," he said, passing over the flowers into my arms, "oh, and this too." He added a card in a cream envelope and placed it on top of the stems.

Not giving me a chance to question him, he turned and left me standing in the doorway holding them awkwardly.

Closing the door, I went to the kitchen so I could put the flowers in water. There was only one person that had ever bought me flowers and butterflies fluttered in my stomach as I thought about what the card would say.

You wouldn't send anyone flowers if you were unhappy with them, would you? Not a person's favorite flowers, like these. I adored sunflowers. I'd no idea where he got them since they weren't in season in December.

Carefully placing the flowers in the vase that the last flowers had come in, I turned to the card. Slowly taking it out of the envelope, I examined the heart on the front. Hearts were a good sign, weren't they?

I think I read that message three times before it really sank in.

Andy,

I wanted to write to you because sometimes I'm not the best with words. It's difficult to know the right thing to say. Usually when I'm around you, I don't have that problem. With you I know I can say anything and you won't judge me for it because you know what I really mean to say.

I hurt you and I'm sorry.

When I asked for a bit of time to get myself together, I don't think either of us expected it to take this long. You were incredibly patient and I took advantage of that. It was too easy for me to push away all the things I needed to do in order to be the man that I need to be, for you. At some point, I think I stopped really trying, fearing that it was too much to deal with.

This whole time we should have been spending time together. Having dates, hanging out with friends. All that you'd said you wanted. Just being around you makes everything better. I don't think you know how special you are.

Even when you asked me to let you in, rather than seeing you becoming frustrated, I hid away further. I went about this all wrong. Instead of tackling all my issues myself, or with Dr. Arnold's help, I should've told you about it. About how I struggle to trust after being cheated on twice with both of my brothers. About how lonely I've become after cutting off half my family and all of my old friends when they took sides against me.

This weekend I spent time with my brother Alex and worked through a lot of things and rebuilt some bridges. But the worst part of Sunday was hearing that you'd gone out with another man and thinking that you might've given up waiting on me. It was the push that I needed.

You are everything to me. My best friend. I think I've been falling in love with you for a while, and might already be in love with you, but I've been stupid and selfish and kept you at a distance.

That's not what I want anymore. You are what I want. Everything you said you wanted, I need to have with you. Dates, meeting family, being around friends as boyfriends. I want to be with you every day. Falling asleep with you and waking up together. I'd even consider a cat. I just need you, Andy.

You are someone I think I could have a future with and it used to scare me. Now that thought makes me feel light and free in a way that I've never felt before.

You're all that I never knew I needed. Please give us another chance.

If this isn't what you want… if Clara was wrong about Jonas just being a friend, then ignore this and enjoy the flowers. I hope they bring some much needed sunshine.

If you feel the same, agree to a date. Tomorrow. You and me, in a restaurant, having dinner together. Let's do this properly. See if what we had is still there underneath the hurt I caused by pulling away, for not seeing how good this could be.

I've made a reservation. Let me know if I should keep it.

I really am sorry that I caused you pain.

Yours, always,

Will

Putting the card down, I noticed a folded piece of thick paper had fallen out.

Unfolding it, I gasped at the drawing of myself, caught at the moment of laughing at some joke. This was how Will saw me? The guy in the picture was interesting, instantly attracting attention. The kind of guy you wanted to know. He was the type that you wondered what had made him laugh so you could be in on the joke.

When had he drawn this? It was apparent that he had looked at this often. The paper was worn in the corners. This picture was important to Will. I was important to him.

It didn't take me long to make up my mind about what I wanted to do. Sending Will a message, I agreed to the date. Nerves rose, but I pushed them back. If there was one thing I was certain of, it was that Will and I would be great together if we were on the same page.

It looked like we finally were.

Twenty Nine - Andy

It was only when I woke up the next day that I remembered that I didn't have a car and it was still raining from the day before.

I weighed my options but decided if Will wanted to be my boyfriend, I needed to know if I could rely on him. I put that to a test with a call.

The phone rang a couple of times before Will answered warily, "Hey, everything okay?"

"Hey," I blew out a breath, "I need a favor. My car wouldn't start last night and I left it at the office. Could you maybe pick me up on your way in?"

He let out a chuckle, "Phew, I thought you were canceling. Sure thing, babe. I'll text you when I'm there, okay?"

My heart stalled when he so casually called me babe, the endearment tripping easily off his tongue.

"That's, um, yeah, that's great. Thanks, Will." I managed to get out before saying bye and ending the call.

So far, Will was killing it in the boyfriend game.

Practically giddy from the call, it took me no time at all to get ready for work. I even had time to look for a mechanic to fix my car.

Will arrived earlier than I thought and it made me smile to think that he was excited to see me as I was him.

He was standing at the door to the building under a large umbrella and I couldn't resist pressing a kiss to his cheek. "Thanks for this, honey."

I'd never seen Will blush, but pink spread quickly over his cheeks and even to the tips of his ears at my words. It was possibly the most adorable thing I'd ever seen him do, and I vowed to make him blush more. The endearment had slipped out, one that I'd never used before but it just seemed to fit him. He was as sweet to me as honey.

Safe from the rain under the umbrella, Will escorted me to the car, even opening the door for me, making sure I was seated before dashing around to the driver's side.

The car was warm, heated seats all toasty, and I enjoyed the journey to work for the first time in months.

We didn't talk a lot, both seemingly lost in our own thoughts. I wanted to wait to talk about anything on our date, or after it. I didn't want to get too heavy when we had to work all day together.

"I know we have shit to talk about," Will said, proving again we were on the same wavelength, "but I think we should wait until our date. So we can do it properly."

"Funnily enough, I was just thinking the same thing."

Sharing a smile, we merged into the early morning traffic.

My new (maybe boyfriend?) had taken me home at the end of the day after the mechanic looked at my car and then towed it away. While not terribly expensive to fix, the guy didn't have the parts and had to order them. It was unlikely that I'd get my car back until next week.

Will immediately offered to be my ride for as long as I needed him, and I caught Clara giving us funny looks when she overheard. Will noticed and just gave her a smile, which was a total change from before when he hadn't wanted anyone to know anything about us.

The rain had started again, with only a brief reprieve in the afternoon. So Will parked, picked up his umbrella from the back seat, and escorted me to the door.

Leaning down, he placed a barely there kiss on my lips. Unable to resist, I pushed up on my toes to capture his lips as he pulled back. Our next kiss was firmer, bolder, but neither of us pushed for more than that.

Pulling away, his chocolate eyes dancing with joy, "Later, baby. I'll pick you up at seven."

Wanting to tease Will, I dressed for our date in a pair of gray slacks that were cut perfectly. My butt looked damn good in them, if I did say so myself. I paired them with a white button down that had tiny gray birds embroidered on it.

Will arrived early and I buzzed him up while I splashed on some of my favorite cologne and attempted to locate my keys and phone. He looked utterly delectable in navy slacks and a light blue shirt. Somehow the blue brought out his olive skin and made his eyes pop.

He kissed me when I invited him in to wait and I was tempted to cancel our dinner plans in favor of staying in and peeling him out of those clothes.

The way his eyes darkened as he scanned me from head to toe suggested that I wouldn't have to work too hard for that to happen. His groan as I turned around to pick up my phone made me laugh. He was already putty in my hands.

Thirty - Will

If Andy leaned over one more time, showcasing that amazing bubble butt in those pants, then I wouldn't be held accountable for my actions. As it was, I had to adjust myself, my tight pants strangling my hardening dick.

Andy turned to me. "I'm ready, honey," he said and started to lead me out.

Honey. I'd never been one for pet names and was as shocked as Andy when "babe" slipped out this morning. Having him call me honey just did something to me, warmed me deep inside. It felt like he belonged to me, as much as I belonged to him, and the name just showed it to everyone who might hear us.

I couldn't help but reach for his hand as we walked to the elevator. Inside, I drew him into a hug, my eyes burning as I took a breath full of the scent of his hair.

"Thank you. For giving us a second chance," I whispered into his ear, feeling him shudder and just melt into me.

He clutched at my back, "Thank you for wanting a second chance." The words were quiet, said against my neck.

We broke apart when the elevator reached the ground floor, but I needed to be touching him, so I reached for his hand again.

Seeming to know that I needed the simple show of affection, he rested a hand on my thigh as I drove.

I tried to start the conversation, get the heavy stuff out of the way, but Andy insisted we leave it until we were at the restaurant.

"I just want to enjoy being with you now. Oh, and have dinner, I'm starving!"

***

Dinner passed in no time, and while we talked about some of the issues that kept us apart, a lot of it Andy insisted that he would find out over time, we just had to learn to communicate better. When the mood turned serious, he'd told me about the abuse that he'd suffered in the past and that arguments might trigger a fight or flight response. I was his first relationship since Jason, the worst of his exes, so he couldn't be sure how he'd react. Since I'd already decided to continue with therapy, I assured him that I'd discuss with Dr. Arnold ways to communicate when we disagreed without triggering him. Maybe he could join me in therapy when he was ready or if he needed it.

His ability to forgive and forget astounded me. I was truly floored at his capacity for kindness. I'd been beating myself up for hurting him and here he was, ready to forgive me and just move forward.

"I don't deserve you," I told him seriously.

"You can't think like that. Everything that happened is going to make us stronger going forward. We know what not to do now." He squeezed my hand that was resting on his thigh. Going home would be difficult; I didn't want to let go of him now that I finally had him.

If I'd realized how good I'd feel, being loved by Andy, much sooner, I wouldn't have fought it. I felt like I could conquer anything.

Thirty One - Andy

A dinner date was followed by a movie date the next night. Deciding that I needed him in my bed, I insisted on cooking for him the third night, making it clear exactly what I wanted.

Will brought a lovely bottle of wine that we drank while eating perched on the sofa and talking.

Rather than talk everything through on our first date, I'd insisted that he just tell me the really important things, and we could slowly reacquaint ourselves with the other over time.

Discussion over my "date" with Jonas was out in the open at the restaurant the first night, and I'd sent Jonas a selfie of Will and I, copying the pose from the one he sent.

In the spirit of being totally honest and open, I let Will see the messages between me and Jonas. I knew he would never have asked, but I wanted to reassure him that he had absolutely zero competition there.

The celebratory gif that Jonas had replied with had Will and I cracking up at the table.

We'd also gone over some of my dating history, again just in the spirit of being open and honest. Will had told me how proud he was of me to get through such a difficult situation and come out unjaded. There were lingering feelings of shame from putting up with it for so long, but at the time I'd felt trapped by circumstances. I suppose I'd come out of the whole thing stronger.

Will had a lot of baggage, but over time we would work through it - as a team, instead of him dealing with it on his own.

At my apartment, the atmosphere was different, filled with expectation. We both knew what was coming. I was totally putting out on the third date.

We started making out on the sofa. Just kissing for the sake of kissing, but it wasn't long before hands started to wander and we began to peel each other out of our clothes.

"Bed, now." I panted.

We toppled into bed, mouths still fused, but with all of our clothing on the floor. Moving up the bed, I reached for the lube that I'd left out, desperate for Will inside me. We could take it slowly next time, but I needed him now.

I slicked up a couple of fingers and went to start prepping myself when Will stayed my hand.

"This time, would you fuck me?" he asked, his voice husky and full of desire.

"You want that?" I asked, shocked.

"Yeah, is that okay? Do you top?"

"Um," I blushed, "I've never done it. I don't want to hurt you."

"I'd like to be your first, if you want to try it. There's nothing I want more than the feeling of you deep in me."

I nodded and drew him into a kiss, before pushing him back against the pillows so I could cover him with my body. I rutted against him, my cock stiff against his hard length, causing us both to gasp and moan in pleasure.

Working my way down his body, I kissed and licked at him, drinking in his moans.

Finding the lube as I reached his cock, I licked and sucked the crown before deciding to open him up with my mouth before stretching him further with my fingers.

Licking over his balls, sucking each one in turn, I pushed his legs back so that I could get to my prize. Feathering my tongue gently over his hole, I felt Will shudder and then heard him beg, "More."

Kissing and sucking at his hole until I felt it soften, I used my tongue and a wet finger to slowly open him to me. Really taking my time, I ate at him, pushing my tongue as deep as it would go. Reveling in the taste of him, soap, something that was just Will, and musk.

He started to beg again, demanding more and I stretched a hand out for the lube, Will passed it to me. One lubed finger quickly became two as I sucked his cock deep into my mouth, letting him into my throat and swallowing around the head. His moans became frantic, letting me know he was close.

I'd happily have him find his release in my throat, but the idea of fucking him was too good to pass up. I really needed to be inside him. Adding a third finger and scissoring them to stretch him properly, I sucked and kissed slowly up his gorgeous body, sharing the taste of his pre-cum in a filthy kiss.

"Now…Please." he rasped.

"Condom?"

"No. Inside. Now"

Assuming he had bottomed before, I didn't ask him to turn over to make it easier. I wanted to see his expression as I pushed into him for the first time.

Covering my cock in lube, I positioned the tip at his stretched hole and pushed in slowly.

It was nearly over before it began. The tight heat that hugged my shaft perfectly was overwhelming and I had to pause and pull firmly on my balls to keep from exploding.

Ever so slowly, I inched in further until I was fully seated inside him. Will reached for me and I leaned down to kiss him, allowing him a moment to adjust before I began to rock gently.

Slow, careful thrusts followed and everything else ceased to exist but this moment. Time was irrelevant, just the feeling of us being joined in the most intimate of ways, staring into each other's eyes as I filled him.

Eventually, Will needed more and wrapped his legs around my hips, his feet pushing on my ass to go deeper, harder, and faster.

Sweat slicked our bodies and the room was filled with the scent and sounds of sex. I never wanted to stop pushing inside him; feeling him clenching around my cock had me barreling towards my release.

His cock was slick with pre-cum and each thrust inside him had my stomach rubbing against it. He panted against my neck, "So good. Close." and I went harder, pushing as deep as I could go. I changed the position of his hips, tilting them slightly and hit his gland, causing him to cry out.

Over and over, I aimed my thrusts at the spot until he came, shooting spurt after spurt over his chest, cum hitting his chin.

So close to my own orgasm, I couldn't help but follow him as his muscles clamped down on my cock. It seemed to go on forever as I filled him, just rocking gently and trying to breathe.

We enjoyed the high, bodies intertwined, kissing gently before I softened and started to slip out of him.

I looked down and groaned, "That's so hot." as I watched my cum leak from his abused hole. Running my finger down his crack, I gathered some and pushed it back into him, rubbing his rim gently with a wet finger.

"You like that, huh?" he sounded amused and completely wrecked, his voice hoarse.

"My cum in you…yeah."

"Hmm, I think you just discovered a new kink, babe."

"I think you might be right, honey."

I spent the next little while just stroking him and pressing kisses wherever I could before finally helping him clean up and get ready to sleep.

We wrapped around each other in the same way we did at the cabin. It felt natural and perfect, the knowledge that he'd still be with me in the morning made joy bubble inside me. I'd never slept better.

Thirty Two - Will

Andy's apartment was usually on the cooler side, but when I woke the next morning it was bitterly cold and I could see our breaths fogging around us in the air.

"Andy, sweetheart. You need to wake up." I ran my fingers through his hair, pushing it off his sweet face. My fingertip traced along his eyebrows and I placed a kiss on the crown of his head.

Our body heat seemed to be the only thing keeping Andy sleeping so soundly and I hated to have to wake him but it was getting uncomfortably chilly in the apartment. The heat must be out.

Andy woke with a shudder and tried to burrow into me, pulling the covers tighter around us.

"Damn, it's freezing! Fuck! The heat must be on the fritz again!" His teeth chattered.

Unable to see him suffering, I leapt out of bed and threw on my discarded clothes from the night before, including my coat and scarf.

"Where do you keep sweats and hoodies?" I asked, eyeing the room.

Andy pointed to the closet and I found the thickest pair of sweats, some fluffy socks, t-shirt and a warm looking sweater. He raised an eyebrow at the lack of underwear but said nothing, dressing quickly under the covers.

Getting out of bed, he walked to the bathroom and ran the tap, "Yep, no hot water either. Fuck, it's too cold for this shit!"

I went to him and drew him into a hug. "Look, it's still early. Pack a bag for a couple of days, you can come stay with me. We've got time to go to my place and shower before work if we're quick about it."

He stared at me, astounded. "You want me to come stay? Just like that?"

"Absolutely. I told you, I'm all in now. I love you and want you with me. You can't stay here. December weather and no heat at home don't mix."

His mouth dropped open. "You love me?"

"I do."

"I love you too, Will."

His lips slammed into mine before softening their brutal assault into a tender kiss. Just when we were in danger of getting carried away, he shivered and I pulled back.

"We need to get you somewhere warm." I told him softly.

"Could you help me pack, please? I really want a shower, and I imagine you feel a bit gross." he gave a laugh and made a face.

Scrunching my face as I realized how crusty I felt, I gave him a nod. "Shower for sure."

Together, we packed quickly, stuffing a weekend's worth of clothing into a bag while Andy put a call in to his landlord. The older man assured him he would do his best to get it fixed as quickly as possible. It seemed it was just Andy's apartment that was having issues with no heating or hot water.

"You know, these things come in threes," he mused. "At least, that's what my mom always said."

"Mine says that, too. Let's hope it's already happened and you missed it."

It'd be a relief to get into my building where it was warm. The car journey wasn't long enough to properly thaw us out after so long in the cold of Andy's apartment.

While in the car I remembered the promise I'd made to Gem. "Sweetheart, do you still have Gem's number?"

"Uh, I think so. Why?"

"Go text her and say; hashtag Andill has set sail. She'll want to have coffee with us soon, if that's okay with you?"

"Andill?"

"She ships us, remember? That's our ship name."

Laughter burst from him. "That's amazing! Love it!"

We didn't have to wait long for the reply or demand for a coffee double date. Gem wanted us to meet her new man.

"D'you think Henry would mind us meeting up with Gem?" Andy wondered.

"Dunno, we could run it by him first before we set it up?"

"Good idea."

The distance between our apartments wasn't much but the freezing weather outside made me grateful for the car. Parking in my assigned spot next to Alex's car in the guest slot, I led Andy up to reception. At the attendant's desk, I greeted the person on duty, offering them my I.D and asking them to allow access for Andy as my partner. Notifying them that he'd be staying, I asked if it was possible to get a key made.

Andy looked shocked when he was told he'd have a key by the end of the day. Maybe I was moving too fast for him, but I didn't want to go slow now. I was prepared to show him that he was at the center of my life. Everything was just about making him happy.

"Will," He started to say.

I turned him to face me, so he could look me in the eyes and see how serious I was about this. "All of my life is open to you. You need somewhere to stay, my place is yours. I want you to be able to come and go as you please. It's important to me, so please? Take the key when it's ready?"

Nodding, he wrapped his arms around me and took a juddering breath, pushing down the emotion I'd seen welling in his eyes.

We took the elevator to my home on the sixth floor, my arm wrapped around him the whole time as he got himself together.

I gestured for him to follow me to the kitchen, "Coffee?"

"Please" he said quietly, still overwhelmed. We'd talk more after coffee and a shower.

Alex called out from the kitchen, "Just made a pot." and took his cup through to the dining nook where we'd put the new table. After putting his cup down, he approached Andy with his hand out to shake. "Hey, you must be Will's boyfriend. Andy, right? I'm Alex, Will's brother."

Andy looked stunned but still shook Alex's hand before clumsily dropping onto a seat at the table. "Hi, Alex. Nice to meet you."

"Sorry, sweetheart. I forgot to say Alex would be here this morning."

Clearly worried that he was coming off as rude, Andy roused from his shock. "Sorry, Alex. It's been a strange day already. How're you? You settling in okay here?"

Leaving them to chat, I went to get Andy some coffee and see what there was for breakfast. Andy needed food in him soon or he'd get hangry. I'd heard the others in the office joke about it before when Andy'd been on the warpath after missing lunch. My man was a grouch when he got hungry.

Finding some pastries, I put them on a plate and took it and Andy's mug of coffee over to him. He was making Alex laugh at a work anecdote. A feeling of rightness stole over me at seeing them get along so well and so quickly after meeting.

Sharing a shower to save time was intimate and sweet. Also frustrating because there was no time for anything other than washing each other. This would just make it better later, when I could take my time exploring his body, mapping it with my tongue.

Back in the car for the ride to work, Andy seemed lighter. Like having breakfast with my brother had been the final piece in the puzzle that was our relationship.

"So you talked to your brother about me?" He asked, breaking his silence.

"I did. Is that okay? I watched him nod out of the corner of my eye, not willing to take my attention off of the slippery roads. The rain of the day before had turned to ice with the overnight frost.

"Alex suggested that I include the drawing."

"That was his idea? I love how you see me." His voice broke. "I'm so happy that I agreed to that date."

"So am I, love."

Thirty Three - Andy

In the space of less than a day, Will had blown my mind by letting me top, telling me he loved me - first, no less. Then he'd insisted I stay with him all weekend! I thought I was going to cry when he asked for a key to be made for me. It was so thoughtful of him, making sure I felt free to come and go as needed.

I don't think Will could really grasp how messed up some of my relationships had made me. So this idea of having freedom was amazing. It wasn't just that I could come and go. It was the idea that he wanted me around and was sharing his space with me.

Meeting his brother was a big deal to me but they were both so casual about it. Alex was important to Will. They were only just re-establishing their bond but I knew that Will would pick me over Alex. I came first to him. It was there in how closely he stood, his hand on the small of my back. In the way he sat close at breakfast, making me take first pick of the food.

Still, I relished the chance to meet his family. I'd been hidden away before. Kept a secret. Jason didn't have anyone close to him, which looking back, had been a red flag. So Will openly talking about me, seeking his brother's advice, made my heart melt. If I hadn't already fallen for him, this would've pushed me over the edge.

"When we get to work, I think we should visit HR and tell them about us." Will suddenly suggested, "I know it isn't against the rules, but I don't want to hide what we have. We did that before. Or rather, I told you to hide us." he paused, "I want this to be a proper fresh start. So that I can give you all that you said you wanted."

"And what was that?" I teased. "Other than your dick, I mean."

He laughed but quickly sobered. "Dates, friends, family, as boyfriends.

My heart stuttered in my chest, "Will…I just wanted you. That's all that matters to me. I don't want to force you to do things just to make me happy."

"The thing is, this is making me happy. I want to tell everyone that you're mine. My inner caveman wants to claim you so everyone can see that you belong to me. I want our colleagues, friends and family to see that you love me and I love you. You aren't forcing me to do a thing, babe."

"I love that."

"What?"

"The way you call me babe, or sweetheart, or love. It's the best feeling when I hear it."

"Which is why we have to tell HR so we can be open at work."

"They're going to lose their shit."

***

There was a new guy in the HR department and oh my God was he fine! I caught Will looking at me as we explained our situation and Korain, the new HR administrator, found us the appropriate forms.

In the elevator, Will smirked. "You're practically drooling. I'm glad we sorted stuff out before you saw Korain. He's like something out of that k-pop group you like."

I laughed, but blushed. Busted. Korain was totally my type. "He's got nothing on you, babe." I told him before pressing a quick kiss on his lips.

"Hmm."

I got the feeling that he was teasing me. A small smile curved the corners of his lips, but I still tried to soothe him. "No, really. I can see that he's gorgeous but that's all it is. All I need is you."

"I trust you. I don't easily trust, but with you...there's no question. I know you'd never hurt me like that."

After kissing me breathless in the elevator, we announced our relationship to our teams by walking in holding hands before Will went to the break room to get us coffee. Handing me mine, he kissed the top of my head before sitting down and starting his day.

Most of the staff just gaped at us and I couldn't hold back my laughter. Giving Will a shove, I got his attention and motioned to the office watching us.

"Andy and I are a couple. Deal with it." Will said in his usual brusque work tone. It was so hot when it wasn't directed at me.

Freddie appeared in the doorway, "Show's over, everyone. Back to work please, I'm sure there's work to be done." There was laughter in his voice.

Coming over to us, he whispered, "Just heard the news. About time, you two!" He clapped us both on the shoulder and left again.

"Well, at least the company's on board." I whispered.

A few minutes later Will's phone buzzed on the desk. Glancing at it, he gave a laugh and showed it to me. The text was from Freddie, saying that his dad had won the bet.

"Bet?"

"Seems they'd bet on how long it'd be before we got together. Parker Senior won since he had inside eight months," he told me, reading the full message and texting back and forth with Freddie.

I shrugged. "I'm just glad neither one of us has to leave."

At lunchtime I got a call from Mr. Grady, my landlord, from my apartment. "Not good news, I'm afraid. You need a new boiler and I can't get one put in until next week. I can give you some space heaters and change out your shower for an electric shower, it'll heat the water for you. It's the best I can do for you. I'm really sorry, Andy. You're a great tenant and you've fixed the place up nice."

"Can't be helped, it isn't your fault, Mr. Grady."

"Alan, please, you've known me long enough."

"No worries, Alan. You've done your best. We both know that the boiler's been a bit funny for a while. I have a place to stay for the weekend…"

Will interrupted, "For as long as you need."

"I have a place to stay but wouldn't say no to the new shower. The water pressure isn't great in the current one."

"Say no more, my boy. The electric shower should help with pressure issues. It'll be fitted today and if you need to come home, let me know, and I'll drop off those heaters to you until the new boiler is installed next week."

"Thanks, Alan."

Ending the call, I turned to Will, kissing him on the cheek. "You're the best boyfriend."

"Anything for you."

I knew he meant it.

Thirty Four - Will

Having Andy in my bed was amazing! Waking up to him after a night of scorching hot sex was better. I could have done without my four-year-old nephew bursting in, though.

"Uncle Will! Daddy showed me my new bed. It has dinosaurs on it!" he announced running around to my side of the bed.

I'd picked out the set on the way home from work earlier in the week. I wanted my place to feel like a home away from home for him.

Pulling the covers over Andy a bit more since we were naked, I turned over to face Joe. "Really? So cool."

"Uncle Will, is that Uncle Andy in bed with you?" the little man asked.

Lowering my voice, I said "It is, but he's still sleeping so you need to be very quiet, okay?" I waved Joe away so I could get up and dressed. We had plans to take him to the zoo today and Andy was nervous about it.

Once he left, Andy turned over. "Uncle Andy?" His eyes were wide and filled with tears.

I drew him into my arms and let him cry it out. It was all a bit too much for my sweetheart. He'd given me bits and pieces of his history as he sobbed in my arms, so I knew these were healing tears, not ones of sadness. I was showing Andy what he meant to me by fulfilling promises, loving him openly and being there for him. Having that love and support would lessen the damage of those emotional scars over time.

There was a commotion from the living room and I heard feminine voices as well as my brother and nephew.

"Andy, sweetheart…um…I think my mom is here. My sister, too. Are you okay to meet them?"

He launched himself into sitting up. "Now? Like right now?"

"Sounds like it. You can go have a shower first if you like. We need to get a move on, we're booked at the reptile house."

I watched as he took a deep breath, visibly calming. "I'll take a quick shower and come meet them after. I don't want your mom to see me for the first time with bedhead." He gave a little laugh, but it was forced and sounded strangled.

Cupping his chin, I pulled him to me, pecking a kiss to those lovely full lips. "Mom'll love you. I promise. Even if she hates you, I won't stop loving you. Mom will just have to deal with it."

Andy's eyes filled again but he shook them away.

"Oh, and Matilda is a pushover. Just call her Matty, not her full name. She loathes Tilly, so only call her that if you want to piss her off."

He laughed. "Got it." Climbing out of bed, he gave me a wink when he caught me staring at his beautiful behind and shook it a little with a chuckle at my groan.

Pulling on some sweats and a t-shirt, I ran my hands through my hair in an attempt to look presentable for my family.

I found them sitting around the new table, Joe cuddled with his nana, and Mom patting Alex's arm. Matty sat on the couch chatting on her phone but gave me a wave as I went by.

"Hey Mom," I said, kissing her cheek and settling into the seat next to her, "are you coming with us today?"

"If you don't mind, I'd love to. Alex says you have your young man staying with you and I just had to come meet him! He sounds wonderful darling, I'm so happy for you."

She pulled back to take me in properly. "I don't think I've seen you look so content. Happiness suits you."

Smiling at the thought of Andy, I said, "I've never felt like this, Mom. It's different this time."

We chatted for a while and I began to get worried that Andy was too nervous to come join us. Just when I was about to go and get him, I heard him approach.

"Hey, Matty. Nice to meet you." he said to my sister.

"Hey, Andy. Same." She said with a friendly smile, pulling her phone from her ear for a second.

Heading over to him, I wrapped an arm around him and led him over to my mom to make the introductions.

Andy seemed at a loss but Mom motioned him to come closer. Reaching up and with him leaning down, she grasped his face. "William, you didn't tell me how handsome Andrew was!" Kissing both of his cheeks, making him blush a furious red, she said, "Welcome to the family, darling boy."

As I expected, they hit it off immediately and I was sure that I'd live to regret how close they became after just one day.

While Andy was subdued around my brother, he was adorable with my nephew, managing to keep Joe engaged in the exhibits by telling him all manner of strange facts. He even worked a miracle and got Matty interested in what we were seeing rather than what was on her phone.

With Mom, he was charming. They chatted together over lunch and teased me mercilessly. Not that I minded (much), I was just happy to have almost all of my favorite people together.

***

After our weekend together, even with as busy as my apartment was, I couldn't bear to think about Andy going back to his place. My head kept reminding my heart that I was moving too fast and asking him to stay - permanently - was a bad idea.

Andy had gotten the call late Monday that his apartment wasn't ready, there'd been a delay. It bought me a few more days with him. By the end of the week though, there was a shiny new boiler and he could go home.

My heart felt heavy at the thought of him not being here every day. I almost asked to go with him but didn't want to come off clingy. After our starts and stops, I didn't want any distance between us.

So on our last night together I'd just soaked in the peace that I got from being with him. Andy had settled here and it felt so natural to sleep next to him. We slept as we usually did, wrapped around each other.

The next night sleep wouldn't find me. My bed was empty without him in it. I'd lain awake for hours until exhaustion had taken over.

I dragged myself through the day, spending time with Alex and Joe and helping Alex house hunt once Joe was safely tucked up in bed.

When I tried to sleep again, it wouldn't come. I passed miserable hours tossing and turning knowing that it was Andy that I needed so I could sleep. Giving up in the early hours of the morning, I got up and walked the few blocks to his apartment. Andy met me at the door to his building, on his way to my place, and we laughed at how pathetic we were being. We couldn't manage two nights apart.

Later, tucked up and sleepy in Andy's bed he asked, "Will?"

"Hmm?"

"I was thinking."

"About what?"

"Um…How about, just hear me out okay?" He wiggled to get free and sat up against the headboard, his face serious. "I've loved being at your apartment and want to wake up to you all of the time."

"I want that, too."

He smiled, "Good, so we're on the same page there. I think, now this is just a suggestion." holding his hands up in a placating gesture."I love sleeping next to you and knowing you'll be there in the morning.

"So, I think we should move you into my apartment until my lease is up. There's only a couple of months left. In the meantime, Alex could stay at your place and use that time to find somewhere for himself and Joe. I'd stay at yours, but it got awfully crowded there at the weekend. Alex could've had my place but there's no place for Joe."

Considering his idea for a moment, I said, "That's a great idea, baby." I pulled him to me so I could kiss him. Breaking apart, I said, "I can't wait to live with you."

 "Even if it's really quick?"

"It doesn't feel like it. Maybe officially we've only been together nearly two weeks, but we had all those months of hookups and then being friends. We just work. All we can do is try it. If we need a break from each other, I can always go back to my place."

"So we're doing this?"

"We are."

Epilogue

Andy

The months passed with Will and I living together in my tiny apartment. While less than ideal, it taught us a lot about each other. We were in sync about cleaning and clutter, but Will was a night owl and I loved the dawn.

It was an adjustment, but we made it work.

There were arguments, but we learned how to communicate better for it, and making up was always an experience. One really bad fight had us sleeping apart for the first time in months and it had proven to be a miserable night. Sleep deprived, Will had appeared at our door with flowers and a drawing, though he'd had nothing to apologize for. Dr. Arnold gained another patient that day, since it was my issues that'd caused the spat.

What didn't change was the love we held for each other. If anything, it got deeper as we became more secure in what we had.

Sex with someone who truly loved you? Couldn't be beaten but we were more than that now.

Will was my best friend, my lover, and about to be my husband.

After a hectic Christmas at Alex's new home with his family, including a very subdued Charlie, Abby and Josh, we decided to go away for New Year's to the cabin, just the two of us.

In the new year, we moved into Will's apartment and it was bittersweet for both of us to let my place go. We needed the extra space, so it made sense to move, but my old apartment held so many good memories for us.

Will insisted that we take the couch after all the work Abby had put into making it look good. That went a long way in making her accept him. So had the way he had nursed me through a bout of the flu, tenderly taking care of me for days before he became ill with it himself. His mom stepped in then to look after "her boys".

Abby and Will were a work in progress, but I knew it was because of the way he'd treated me in the past, rather than now. I'd never been so well-loved and my sister could see that. Over time she'd learned to love him as a brother.

We'd met up with Gem a few times and were happy to see her settled with her new guy, but out of loyalty for our friends, we didn't meet up with her again after that. It'd been nice, but a little uncomfortable when Gem's man had asked how we knew her.

The day I moved in officially, Will got on one knee and asked me to marry him, which had ruined my plan of proposing at his building's rooftop garden under the stars. When I produced a ring for him from my pocket, he made me promise to pretend his proposal hadn't happened and to go through with my plan.

So that night, even though he was expecting the question, I still surprised my fiancé with a romantic proposal and engagement party, slash house-warming, with our friends and family on the rooftop of our building, under a curtain of stars.

Will

Life with Andy had surpassed anything I could've dreamed up. My fiancé was passionate, loving and loyal. The way his brain worked fascinated me. He was absolutely my favorite person in the world.

Over the months there were ups and downs like with any couple, but for every bump in the road, there were a hundred nights of pure joy. Simple things like cooking dinner with him became treasured memories.

We celebrated Andy's thirtieth by booking our favorite bar for the night and my relationship with Charlie had improved enough by then that he made an appearance at the party. He didn't stay, too fresh from rehab to be around so much temptation, but he spent some time with Andy giving him a gift of a photograph he had taken of me and Andy at Christmas while we weren't looking. In it, we're just gazing at each other, ridiculously in love and in our own world. That photo, in its handmade driftwood frame, sits on our coffee table for everyone to see.

Andy wanted all of my family at our wedding, so I made an effort with Charlie, despite past hurts, it wasn't that hard to let it go. Being truly happy with Andy made it easy. Charlie had made many mistakes and had paid for them all. We'd nearly lost him for good and it would've haunted me forever having so much unresolved between us.

It seemed like a great idea to spring a destination wedding on Andy. Mexico had started out as a much needed holiday, but I'd been looking at places to stay and spotted a destination wedding resort. Andy had been stressing about planning a wedding, so this was perfect. They did everything for us and we could just enjoy it.

Keeping it from him had been difficult. We didn't keep secrets from each other, about anything, but I knew he would appreciate it. I'd planned everything and sworn everyone to secrecy until we got there. Andy had no idea our families were coming, too. He thought it was just the guys.

When we arrived, I'd gotten down on one knee and he'd tried to laugh me off, becoming serious when he saw the others watching with bated breath.

"Andrew Barker, I'd already agreed to marry you, but we never set a date. How about you marry me, here, in three days' time?"

He looked like he'd stopped breathing, then he let out a shout. "Seriously? Here? Yes!"

I'd never loved anyone more and I couldn't wait to spend the rest of my life with him.

Surrounded by our families and our closest friends, I married my best friend and the love of my life on the beach in Mexico at sunset. A perfect start to a lifetime of love.

Want More?

Andy and Will are back in the next book of the Second Chances series. Twins James and Jayden take a second shot at saving their relationship as Jayden gives James the help he needs to find love.

Want to know what happened with Charlie? Don't worry, he gets his own book and his man. Coming soon.

About the Author

Jax Stuart is a Scottish born author and mum of two kids. She has always wanted to write but nearing a big birthday gave her the boost to finally turn that dream into reality.

Why M/M romance? After reading so much of it over the last couple of years, that's just how the stories and characters came to her.

The queer book community is diverse, inclusive and supportive, allowing all sorts of stories and writers thrive.

When she isn't writing, Jax is studying English Literature, reading all the books she can, spending time with family and friends and cuddling her cats.

You can find her on;

Bookbub, Facebook and Goodreads. Come join her reader group - Stuart's Syndicate.

Printed in Great Britain
by Amazon